# KEEP YOUR ENEMIES CLOSER

MARK O'NEAL

# Keep Your Enemies Closer

Book design by Maureen Cutajar
www.gopublished.com

Printed and bound in USA

# Chapter 1

Gabrielle and I were sitting in first class on our flight to Chicago for Stephanie's wedding that was taking place on Saturday. Gabrielle was one of her bridesmaids, and the two them had gotten really close over the last couple of years. They had decided to bury the hatchet after I got shot on that faithful day at a gas station near Brentwood, CA three years prior; and we regularly saw Stephanie and her fiancé at least once every month or so for the last year. She was marrying a partner at a financial services firm, and she was the happiest I've ever seen her.

I had to admit to myself that seeing Stephanie marrying someone else was a little weird for me even though our relationship had been over for sometime, and the fact that she was now Gabrielle's new best friend was even weirder. I wasn't jealous of Stephanie's new relationship or anything remotely close to that, but I still cared enough about her to wonder if she was making the right decision for herself. Her fiancé Brendan Moss seemed like a legit guy on the surface, but something didn't feel right to me about him. He was too perfect in my opinion—he always seemed to say the right thing to her as though it was scripted, they never had an argument in the two and a half years they dated, and he bought her flowers at least once a week. I thought it was a cool thing for Brendan to buy Stephanie flowers every week—but a thoughtful gesture like that could lose value if it's done too often and might be taken for granted after a while in my opinion.

I befriended Brendan because I really wanted to know what his true intentions were, and whenever Gabby and Stephanie were out shopping or getting their hair and nails done, we were usually on the golf course or at a sports bar throwing back beers. I had a lot more time on my hands once I retired after the 2011-12 NBA season. Malik was traded to Los Angeles the same year I had to work my way back from a long, strenuous rehabilitation that lasted almost half of the season. My life was never the same after being in a coma and nearly dying, and my body had begun to break down with nagging injury after nagging injury robbing me of my explosiveness on the hardwood. I ultimately decided to go out on my own terms rather than be pushed out of the league.

I wanted to be wrong about him because he made Stephanie so happy, but I also felt that things were too good to be true at that point. A person can only fake it for so long before the truth comes out.

"Would you two like something to drink?" the flight attendant asked.

"Sure, I'd like a Miller Draft," I answered.

"What about you, sweetie?" the flight attendant asked Gabrielle.

"I'll just have a bottled water, please," she answered.

"Coming right up," the flight attendant said.

"Getting an early start, huh, baby?" Gabrielle asked.

"I guess you can say that," I answered. "I'm not fully on board with this, Gabby."

"We talked about this...give Brendan a chance."

"I am giving him a chance, but I still don't trust this dude, though. I know his type...mister smooth... mister perfect. He's definitely hiding something, but I haven't been able figure it out yet. I just don't want to see Steph get hurt."

"I don't want her to get hurt, either. You really need to lighten up, and if I didn't know any better, I'd think you still wanted her for yourself."

"Come on, Gabby, you know I only have eyes for you. I can't believe you're saying this after what we did last night, and if you don't believe me, I'll give you an encore performance tonight."

"I'm just messing with you, damn...you have no sense of humor. I know you just want what's best for her, but you have to let it go, boo."

"Okay, I'll let it go...for now."

"Good, I want us to enjoy ourselves this weekend. Put your feelings aside for one day, and I'll give *you* an encore performance you'll never forget."

"Be careful, babe, that's how we got Alexa."

"You once said you could handle ten kids if we had them, remember?"

"Yeah, I remember. The question is, can you handle it?"

"Yes, I can handle ten kids and manage my restaurant with no problem."

"That's my superwoman...."

"And don't you forget it."

The flight attendant brought us our drinks moments later, and I took a sip of my beer and said, "Malik said they will be in Chicago tonight."

"Are they bringing the baby?" she asked.

"Nah, they're leaving her with the nanny," I answered. "Erin doesn't want Janelle around a lot of people because she's worried about germs."

"That's understandable...I felt the same way about all our kids."

"I think you're both overreacting."

"I disagree...you can never be too careful when it comes to germs. Knowing what I learned in my sanitation class, I'm now afraid to eat in restaurants."

"You're afraid to eat in restaurants? How is that possible, babe?"

"I know it sounds crazy, but I don't trust anybody's restaurant but my own. I'm extra cautious when it comes to health code violations."

"I get what you're saying, and no, it doesn't sound crazy. I saw this movie a couple of months ago, and this guy working in a fast food restaurant spit in a man's burger after the man argued about the first burger being too cold. You just never know what people are doing to your food."

"Exactly, and that's why I'm leery about eating just anywhere."

Janelle was born three months after Alexa, and Janelle was Malik and Erin's first child. Alexa was our third child together—Michael was our first, and Maurice Jr. is the middle child. Jason is our oldest at nine years old, and Gabrielle had him from a previous relationship. All of the children were already in Chicago at their aunt and uncle's house for a few weeks before school was going to start. Gabrielle and I had just gotten back from a vacation in the Virgin Islands so that we could attend Stephanie's wedding.

My sister Nicole was supposed to be one of the bridesmaids, but she couldn't make it because she was the lead attorney in a very important murder trial. I guess Stephanie was still considered a member of the family because she still remained close to everybody.

I, on the other hand, was enjoying retirement and had no plans in the immediate future besides raising my kids while Gabrielle toiled long hours at her restaurant in downtown St. Louis. My barbershop and carwash had run on autopilot since my rookie year, so there wasn't much for me to do besides monitor the books each month. I was offered a gig as an analyst for the St. Louis Wolves, but I turned it down because I needed a mental break from basketball. I wanted to take my life in a new direction—I decided I wasn't going to do anything major until Alexa started preschool. Besides, it was Gabrielle's turn to shine.

I accidentally dropped my beer before I could take another gulp because the commotion in coach startled me. A female flight attendant had screamed hysterically after a tall man with broad shoulders punched a male flight attendant in the face and knocked him to the ground before making his way to the cockpit. I motioned to stop him, but Gabrielle grabbed my arm and shook her head. The man's nationality was ambiguous—he could've been Middle Eastern, Eastern European or from the Mediterranean for all I knew. Suddenly, the male flight attendant entered the first class part of the plane with a bloody nose attempting to grab the man by the shoulder before getting socked in the jaw. He hit the floor unconscious while everyone else on the plane froze in horror.

I couldn't just sit by idly and do nothing. I evaded death numerous times and wasn't going to let some terrorist determine my fate without a fight. I was certain that his mission was to fly this particular plane into a building like the Willis Tower.

I jumped out of my seat and grabbed him before he could enter the cockpit. We wrestled in the narrow space of the aisle—our heads, feet and elbows hitting the seats on both sides of us. Damn, he was strong, I thought. The pilot never peeked out to see what was going on though I'm certain he was terrified as to what was going to happen next.

I managed to gain an advantage by getting on top of him before pummeling his face until my knuckles were bleeding. I made sure he was out cold before I got off of him. His mouth and nose were oozing blood on the floor, and my right hand looked like it went through a meat grinder. I then tried to revive the flight attendant lying on the floor next to the cockpit. I shouted to get the pilot's attention.

"I need some help out here!" I shouted before peeking inside of the cockpit. "Don't shoot...I need a first-aid kit for one of the flight attendants and something to bind this passenger!"

"Here, take this," the pilot said, handing me a first-aid kit and handcuffs. "What happened out there?"

"I think this guy was going to take over the plane by force and kill all of us. One of your flight attendants is hurt really bad, and he hasn't regained consciousness."

"Don't worry, we're about to land very soon."

I turned around and shouted, "Are there any doctors on the plane?!"

"I'm a doctor," a middle-aged man replied.

"I can't tell if he is breathing," I said before placing the handcuffs on the passenger. "Do you want me to give him CPR?"

"Hold fast, I'm coming," the doctor said.

He checked the guy's pulse and checked his airway to see if he was breathing. I finally took a moment to look at the faces of the passengers behind me and at Gabrielle. I saw people who still looked terrified and confused, I also saw looks of admiration, and Gabrielle gave me a smile and a nod of approval.

The flight attendant regained consciousness minutes after the doctor worked on him, and the doctor instructed him to remain on the floor until the plane landed and the paramedics came. The passenger's eyes started fluttering, and I kept an eye on him just in case he wanted to try something else. Fortunately, he continued to lie on the floor in pain and didn't move.

I tried to flex my right hand but could barely move it. I knew then it was a possibility that it might have been broken.

"Let me see your hand, baby," Gabrielle said.

"I hope I didn't break it," I said. "I can't move any of my fingers."

"Can you look at my husband's hand, sir?" she said to the doctor.

"Sure, let me take a look at it," he answered. "From the looks of it, we won't be able to know anything for sure until you get an X-ray. Here, wrap your hand with this ice bag."

"Thanks, doc," I said.

"Don't mention it," he said. "You're Maurice Ousley, aren't you?"

"Yes, I am," I answered. "I'd give you an autograph, but...."

"Don't be silly," he said. "We all owe our lives to you."

"We sure do," Gabrielle interjected. "I'm so proud of you right now."

"I just reacted, that's all," I said. "I just didn't want to die like this...you know...being flown into a building by some lunatic."

"I think we should drive back home after the wedding," Gabrielle said.

"I totally agree with you," I added. "I definitely lost my taste for flying for a while."

# Chapter 2

It was a blazing hot August morning in Sikeston, Missouri. It was a typical Friday—people cashing their paychecks, people wrapping up their workweek and people beginning to stream in off of Interstate 55 because it was the weekend. Lambert's Cafe was famous for their hot *Throwed Rolls*, and it was one of the tourist attractions of the town.

Darius Clinton had bounced around from place to place since being wanted by the FBI, and he had settled in Sikeston for the past six months. His appearance was slightly altered—the ordinarily clean-shaved man with close-cropped hair sported a groomed beard and dreadlocks. He had gone by the alias Darren Bostock, landed a job as a bartender at a local sports bar and rented a studio apartment a couple of blocks away. He had decided to make this quaint town home after being on the run for three years.

He arrived at the bar at eleven thirty to prepare for the lunchtime crowd. He didn't like the small town life at first, but in time it eventually grew on him.

"What's up, Darren?" a female server asked.

"I'm good," he said, still not comfortable with his alias even after three years. "It's starting to pick up already, huh?"

"Yeah, August is one of our busiest months of the year," she said.

"Lemme get settled in here," he said.

"Okay, baby," she said. "Holla if you need anything."

Darius nodded and began to get settled in at the bar. The server's name was Megan McGovern; a single, thirty-four-year-old Irish cocktail waitress with a tattoo of a rose right above her voluptuous right breast. She was an attractive woman who had a crush on Darius because she sensed that he wasn't a local and was intrigued by that fact. However, Darius made it a cardinal rule to never engage in talk about his personal life on any level to anyone, so nobody knew a great deal about him. Nevertheless, his air of mystery made Megan want him even more.

Darius finished settling in; and his first two customers were a white construction worker who was done for the day and a muscular, middle-aged black man who had a salt-and-pepper beard. The black guy had on a black wife beater and black jeans, and he had a tattoo of barbed wire going around his right and left biceps. The construction worker was a regular, but he had never seen the black guy before that afternoon.

"What can I get you, Brandon?" Darius asked.

"Hey, Darren," he answered, "gimme a double shot of bourbon."

"Coming right up," Darius said, "and you?"

"I'll have a Bud Light," the mystery man answered.

"I got you covered," Darius said.

Darius started to make their drinks before a late-breaking story interrupted programming on the HD televisions hanging from the ceiling of the bar. Everyone was glued to the television when the words *Terrorist Attack* were plastered across the screen. The reporter had said the attacker was subdued and that the terrorist had planned on killing the pilot and flying the plane into the Willis Tower. A press conference was moments away.

"Man, what is the goddamn world coming to?" a patron blurted out. "I'm sick and tired of these bastards always trying to blow shit up."

"Yeah, and how the hell do they keep gettin' in the fuckin' country?" another patron asked.

"Here you go," Daruis said, placing their drinks in front of them.

Brandon placed a twenty on the bar, and the other guy followed suit by placing another twenty on the bar. Darius rang Brandon up first, then the other guy before placing their change back on the bar.

"You're not from around here, are you?" the mystery man asked Darius.

"Excuse me?" Darius asked.

"Relax man," he said. "From one hustler to another, I can tell that you're not from around here, that's all."

"You must be mistaken, bruh," Darius said. "I don't know what you're talking about."

"Is everything alright?" Megan asked.

"Everything's fine, Megan," Darius answered.

"Hey, that's Maurice Ousley talking to that reporter," patron 1 said. "That dude must have nine lives."

"He's a bad muthafucka, man," patron 2 said. "Did you see that terrorist's face? He whooped his ass."

"Ain't that the truth, Darius?" the mystery man asked.

"What?" Darius asked. "Who the fuck are you, man?"

"Can we step outside and talk?" the mystery man asked. "I have a business proposition for you."

"I'm working, man," Darius answered. "I really can't talk right now."

"I just want five minutes of your time, that's all," the mystery man said.

"How the fuck do you know me?" Darius asked.

"Not here," the mystery man said.

"Megan, can you cover for me for a few minutes?" Darius asked.

"Sure, honey, go ahead," she answered.

"Make this shit quick, homeboy," Darius said.

"I promise it will be worth your while," the mystery man said.

# Chapter 3

"How does it feel to be a hero, Maurice?" a reporter asked.

"Honestly, I really don't feel like a hero, ma'am," I replied. "I simply reacted when I saw the man knock out one of the flight attendants and head toward the cockpit."

"What was going through your mind when you saw the terrorist heading toward the cockpit?" the same reporter asked.

"I didn't really think," I replied. "Everything was happening so fast, so my first instinct was to lunge at him before he could get to the pilot."

"What stopped you from grabbing him before the flight attendant tried to stop him?" another reporter asked.

"My wife's good sense kicked in, and she held my arm before I could get up," I replied.

The crowd of reporters roared in laughter, and I managed to crack a slight grin after my off-the-cuff reply. I hoped that the barrage of questions was coming to an end—it had been four months since I had spoken to a reporter, and I didn't miss it one bit. I was enjoying living under the radar for a change and cringed at the thought of appearing on more morning talk shows. I tried to shun the spotlight, but I found myself right in the middle of it instead.

I continued to answer questions for another fifteen minutes before heading to the hospital to get my hand X-rayed, and Gabrielle rode in the ambulance with me. I was given a couple of aspirin to ease the pain.

I thought about the first question the reporter asked me when the ambulance left O'Hare Airport. The truth of the matter was I didn't feel like a hero because I didn't want to die for my own selfish reasons. I didn't think about anyone else on that plane other than Gabrielle; and my initial thought wasn't to save the other two hundred or so passengers from the big bad terrorist. An example of a real hero was someone who goes into a burning building to save a mother and her children without regard for his or hers own safety. I beat the guy's ass because it was only one of them, and I felt my chances were good at stopping him. Add another terrorist to the equation, and all bets would have been off.

We spent about three hours at the hospital, and the X-rays were negative. The doctor gave me a prescription for ibuprofen, and then we were on our merry way. We caught a cab to her sister Gina's house because the children were there, and my plan was to visit my old friend Sean later on after I spent some time with the in-laws.

Sean Wilks was just released from prison after serving fifteen years for various drug offenses. I felt I owed my life to him, and I was eternally indebted to him for taking the rap for the entire crew. I haven't seen him in almost three years, so I didn't know what to expect once I saw him again. He had gotten a one-bedroom apartment on the southside of town about a week before we arrived in Chicago.

Gina's husband Rick let me borrow his car to see Sean once everyone finished eating the dinner Gina had cooked. He had an affinity for American sports cars like me, and I often wondered whose car would win in a quarter-mile race—my Challenger or his Mustang. We were going to find out one day soon if I had anything to say about it. Rick and Gina had given me the royal treatment the moment Gabrielle and I got there, and I spent the first hour or so talking about our ordeal on the plane. I left their house fully stuffed and arrived at Sean's apartment on Fifty-Second and Blackstone about an hour later, but I had to circle the block three times before a spot opened up. I've always hated trying to find parking in the Hyde Park neighborhood.

It was about six fifteen in the evening when I stepped inside to be buzzed in. I didn't have to wait but a few seconds, and he met me at the steps on the second floor. We then greeted each other with a firm hug.

"How have you been?" I asked after releasing our embrace.

"I'm great, Maurice," he replied. "Being free feels so surreal, my brother. *Assalaam alaikum.*"

"*Wa alaikum assalaam,* my brother," I said. "I'm so happy you're out, Sean. Sorry I haven't seen you in the last three years. My life has been crazy, and as you may know, our plane was hijacked today."

"Allah has a divine purpose for your life, Maurice, and he will always protect you. What you did today was extraordinary."

"I don't feel like it was extraordinary. I was only thinking about my family and myself on that plane, truth be told."

"Nevertheless, you did the right thing. That's something to be proud of, Maurice."

"Thanks for saying that, Sean. I'm just trying to get back to my old self, but the fact of the matter is I think that person is gone forever."

"All you can do is move forward. Embrace the person you've become."

"That's just it...I don't really know who I am anymore. I used to be a go-getter, but none of this material shit matters to me anymore. Nothing matters but family, and you're family, Sean."

"I can't argue with you...nothing is more important than family. Brothers for life."

"No doubt."

"Hey, the streets were talking for about two months after you got shot. I heard all sort of things about what happened, but I dismissed them because I wanted to hear the truth from you."

"There's nothing really to tell...my wife Gabby's crazy-ass ex-boyfriend shot me because I set him up with the Feds. He actually thought I was gonna help him start a record label because she owed him money. Imagine that?"

"Yeah, that is crazy, man. Did they ever catch up with him?"

"Nah, that fool is still at large as far as I know. That day changed my life forever. What I thought was so important really wasn't important at all in the grand old scheme of things."

"I see...the glitz and glamour doesn't appeal to you anymore, huh?"

"Not at all, bro. I try to stay away from the spotlight if I can help it."

"But it found you anyway...."

"Yeah, unfortunately it did, but I think I can stomach it for a little while longer. Once you've seen the light, everything looks so much clearer."

"The light came on for me when I joined *The Nation*. The drugs, the cars, the money...I realized none of this shit mattered."

"I hear you, but you still gotta live. Here."

I reached in my pocket and handed him five thousand dollars cash in a money clip. I would've given him more if I had more cash on me.

"I can't take this, Maurice," he said. "Allah keeps me fed, my brother."

"Come on, man, I feel guilty enough as it is. I'm not taking that money back."

"Is that why you came to see me? To ease your conscience? You really need to let that shit go."

"If it wasn't for you, my life would be totally different. I owe you."

"No, you don't, Maurice. As of today, you will no longer carry this guilt around with you. I went in with both eyes open...you must have forgotten that I wasn't a naïve little kid when I signed on. I saw an opportunity and I took it...that drug connect was mine, not yours."

"What do you mean? Your wife has moved on, your grown kids are strangers to you, and I can't help but feel somewhat responsible for that."

"Don't, Maurice. This is my burden to bear...I will make amends with my family in due time. Don't worry about me, okay?"

"Alright, I'll let it go."

"So, what else you got going on?"

"I'm here for a wedding...my ex Stephanie is marrying some high society guy...."

"Your ex? Damn, you live an interesting life, man."

"I know, right? We're still cool, but I don't trust the guy she's marrying, though."

"Is there something you're not telling me? You don't still have feelings for her, do you?"

"Nah, it's not like that. This guy seems shady...I don't want her to get hurt, that's all."

"Whatever you say. So, your brother is about to blow up when his rap album drops, right?"

"Yeah, he's in New York recording right now as we speak."

"Cats were playing his shit nonstop in the pen, man. The underground buzz was bananas."

"I'm happy for him. He's having a listening party in about two weeks. You wanna roll?"

"Wish I could...but my PO won't let me."

"Damn, that's right. I'm sorry, Sean."

"Don't even sweat it, man."

"One more thing before I go...."

"What's up?"

"I'm sorry about what happened to Justin...I would've protected him if I could've. The guy who killed him got killed about six months later. I thought you might want to know that his killer didn't get away scot-free."

"I appreciate you telling me this. However, I can't rejoice in another brother losing his life...even if that same brother murder my family."

"I understand. Hey, tell me why they extended your sentence an extra three years?"

"I've been trying to figure that out myself...it was almost like I was set up or something. A random inmate picked a fight with me out of the blue a week before my release, and someone planted drugs in my cell. They tacked on assault and a couple of other bogus drug charges."

"Damn, that's so fucked up."

"Fucked up is an understatement. Those were the longest three years of my life because all I could think of was getting more time tacked on to my sentence again once my release date got closer."

There was brief silence for a moment. I placed the money clip on his coffee table and said, "Alright, I'm out."

"Thanks for stopping by. I'll make sure I cop that CD when it drops."

"Thanks for the support, Sean. See you later."

"Peace be with you, my brother."

# Chapter 4

Darius followed the stranger outside, and they stopped walking once they got to the parking lot behind the bar. Darius looked around to make sure that no one was watching them or listening to their conversation.

"What's this about, man?" Darius asked. "If you came to arrest me, get this shit over with."

"Relax, Darius," the mystery man said. "I'm not here to arrest you."

"Then why are you here?"

"Lemme cut to the chase. My name is Doug Greenwood, and I'm part of a special elite unit that takes out the trash when traditional agencies fail."

"So, you're here to make me an offer that I can't refuse, right?" Darius asked as his blank expression immediately turned into a frown.

"Nah, everybody has a choice, Darius," Greenwood answered. "I'm not here to bust your balls, but you can't run forever. Hell, I used to be just like you...the Feds snatched my ass right out of my house in my boxers without any warning."

"*You* were a player?"

"I was the right-hand man to the biggest player in the Midwest named Stewart Millsap. He and I ran a network called the *Cobras*. We had the police force and the drug game on lock for fifteen years...playing both sides of the fence isn't an easy thing to do. Millsap had to skip town because he let revenge cloud his better judgement, and it cost him everything. I flipped on him in exchange for a lighter sentence...dismantling the organization I helped start. It was either that or spend the rest of my life in federal prison. He's doing life because he killed a cop in cold blood in addition to being a drug dealer. You and me have a lot in common, you know."

"How do you figure that, Greenwood?"

"Both of us wanted to put that asshole we just saw on television in the dirt, and it landed both of us right where you are now."

"Ousley...the worst fucking mistake I could've made in life. I know you're not here because you want me to bring him down...."

"Fuck no, man. As much as I despise his ass, he's not on the America's Most Wanted list. I would've stopped his clock back in the day when I was hustling, but my unit is on the right side of the law and order business."

"Alright, if you don't want me to knock off Ousley, then who?"

"Your cousin, Mike Clinton."

"What? The fuck I am...you might as well take my ass away right now because I'm not doing shit."

"You weren't that hard to find, Darius...just how long do you think it's gonna take the Feds to catch up with you? I got tips on your whereabouts from all over the country every other day...most of them bogus and some legit, but a $50,000 reward is a big motivator, nevertheless."

"I'm not a fuckin' snitch because it goes against everything I believe in."

Darius paused briefly and added, "That's the difference between me and you, Greenwood, and I'm not gonna make my cousin pay for my fuck up. I can live with a life sentence, but I can't live with being a rat."

"I did my homework, homeboy," Greenwood said, cracking a smile. "I knew you would decline my initial offer, so I've got a plan B. Here, listen."

Greenwood pulled out his iPhone and played a recording of

Mike Clinton telling the Feds about loaning Darius his ID and credit card, the drug deal gone bad with the dirty cops in LA, and the murder of Terrence Chandler before stopping the tape. Darius's jaw dropped to the ground when he heard his cousin sell him out with his own ears. His cousin's ultimate betrayal rendered him speechless.

"What do you want to know about that bastard?" Darius finally asked.

"I'd knew you see it my way," Greenwood answered. "Mike buys coke from a guy named Donnie Lucas, and this asshole has been moving tons of weigh every month. Mike is small potatoes compared to this dude, but we need you to come back on the scene and orchestrate a drug deal with the two of them so that we can shut the door on Lucas permanently."

"When do you want to move on them?"

"We'll head out to New York first thing in the morning, and if we bust Lucas; the drug deal at the warehouse in East LA, the murder of Chandler, the shooting of Maurice Ousley at the gas station, and your cousin's association with Lucas will be forgiven. We know that Chandler killed the two cops and the bodyguard because ballistics matched the bullet fragments and shell casings to his gun. Hell, you did us a favor by taking out Chandler after he took out those cops at that warehouse in LA, and Ousley didn't die from you shooting him in the chest."

"Hey, man, I didn't shoot Ousley...you can't pin that shit on me. As for Chandler, he was collateral damage."

"If you didn't shoot Ousley, who did?"

"I have no fuckin' idea. I left town after Ousley tried to set me up with the Feds."

"We just assumed you did it even though witnesses said a masked man shot him in cold blood and fled. He set you up, and you wanted some payback, right?"

"I'm not a stupid man, Greenwood. I admit that I thought about sending him to the afterlife, but I'm not dying to go back to prison. All I wanted to do was get my label back off of the ground, and I was using Ousley to do it because his woman owed me money."

"Drug money, Clinton. We knew you buried that stash somewhere, and I'm willing to bet it was your money that resurrected the record label your cousin is currently running."

"You have no proof of that...."

"Relax, that's not why I'm even here. We want Lucas, and we know that the shipment is coming in this weekend. Help us or else the Feds are eventually going to send you back to prison forever."

"Okay, I'm in, but I don't give a fuck about what you do with Mike."

"Wise decision, bruh. And one more thing...."

"What?"

"Forensics found two different bullet fragments in Chandler's body. Did you have two different guns or was there another shooter?"

"I don't know what the fuck you're talking about, man," Darius lied.

"I knew you say that...but it doesn't matter anyway. Just be ready in the morning...."

"I'll be here."

"You better be."

# Chapter 5

Junior was putting the finishing touches on his first album at a record studio in Brooklyn. He was collaborating with his new best friend, Simon Boston AKA Blaze. They both signed at Rhymes and Lyrics Records at the same time and had been friends every since.

Junior soon realized after his first year of college that school wasn't for him. He decided to pursue his music by buying studio time to record his demo and booking shows as the independent artist known as *Ice Cold* all around Chicago. He was voted as the best new underground rapper in the Chicagoland area, and he landed his record deal about two years later.

Simon's road to success wasn't much different than Junior's—he left Compton and settled in New York to pursue his dream. He also did the underground rap scene and was discovered by Mike Clinton, the CEO of Rhymes and Lyrics Records.

"Man, the track sounds good enough, BJ," Blaze said. "How many times do we have to redo this shit?"

"My rep is on the line, Blaze," Junior answered. "I'm not gonna just put out some bullshit just because I'm tired. This shit is gotta be perfect."

"Fuck this, bruh, I'm hungry as shit. Let's get something to eat."

"Not until I finish this track."

"Suit yourself...I'm gonna get some chicken."

"Where you going? Bring me something back."

"Tasty's...what you want?"

"Some chicken fingers, and bring back some beer."

"Aiight, I got you."

Blaze left, and Junior continued to work on the last track of his album with the engineer. He was about five minutes into it when Mike walked in.

"How's it going?" Mike asked.

"This is gonna be fire, Mike," Junior answered. "I can't wait for this shit to drop."

"I've heard most of it, and you're right. It is fire, son," Mike said. "Saddle up, bruh, your life is about to change."

"That's what's up, man. I'm ready."

"You better be...I got shows booked from now to this time next year. Your first single will be on Hot 97 tomorrow and on MTV Jams next week."

"What?!" Junior shouted, bear hugging Mike. "I can't fuckin' believe this shit! It's finally gonna happen!"

"Believe it, BJ...it's on and poppin', son. I especially like that track *Love N Pain* with Delilah on it...your rap with her vocals is gonna blow up."

"That's the one we're putting out first?"

"Hell yeah...that shit sounds insane."

"That's the lick, Mike. That's my favorite song too."

Junior paused and said, "What about the listening party coming up? Shouldn't we wait until after the party to drop the single?"

"Nah, I don't wanna wait...every day we wait, we lose money. I wanna build that buzz before the album drops."

"Okay, you know what's best."

"Say, where's Delilah at anyway? And Blaze?"

"Blaze went to get some food and drink, and I don't know where Delilah's ass is. I haven't seen her in a couple of days."

"Well, time is money, and I need them to punch the clock. It's time to get this money, man."

"I'm with you, Mike. I waited my whole life for this moment, and I'm not gonna let anything or anyone get in my way."

"That's what I wanna hear, BJ...I wish everybody was as hungry as you are."

Junior gave Mike a fist bump, and Blaze came back with the food and a twelve pack of Corona moments later. Junior pulled out his keys, grabbed a beer and twisted off the cap with his bottle opener. Blaze handed Mike a beer and took a bite of a piece of chicken.

"We can finish up this track tomorrow, Gary," Junior said to the engineer.

"That's cool," Gary said. "See you tomorrow."

Gary grabbed a beer and left, and Junior grabbed a beer and his chicken fingers. Mike took a bite out of a piece of chicken and said to Blaze, "I was just telling BJ that we're gonna drop his first single next week on MTV Jams."

"Track 3?" Blaze asked.

"Yep, and Hot 97 is gonna play it tomorrow," Mike answered.

"That's what's up," Blaze said. "I can't wait until I finish my album...I'm ready for that MTV rotation, too."

"That's just it, bruh," Mike interjected. "If you worked half as hard as BJ here, I'd be bringing out both of y'all...Ice Cold and Blaze at the same damn time. Come on, man, I need you to be on point from now on."

"Okay, Mike, I hear you," Blaze said. "I got three more tracks to lay down, and I'm done."

"Aiight, I need your shit done no later than next week, you feel me?" Mike asked.

"You got it, boss man," Blaze answered.

"I'll see y'all later," Mike said.

Mike left the studio, and Blaze and Junior continued to devour their food and guzzle the beer. Truth be told, Blaze was somewhat of a slacker even though he was just as talented as Junior. Junior was hungry, but Blaze didn't have that same fire. The only reason Blaze actually pursued his rap career was because of a promise he made to his dead friend, Terrence Chandler. Blaze funded his dream with the blood money Terrence left him, but he was starting to lose focus because of the allure of the potential fame and fortune that awaited him.

"What you getting into tonight, fam?" Blaze asked.

"I'm beat, man," Junior answered. "I'mma crash after I get outta here."

"Come on, dawg, let's go to the spot and pop some bottles."

"Nah, fam, let's do it tomorrow. I've been working since seven this morning."

"I feel you, man. I should try to get at Delilah though...she is fine as a muthafucka."

"You wasting your time, man...she ain't checking for no rap dudes. She likes those suit-and-tie brothers and shit."

"How you know that shit?"

"Because I tried to get in them draws, that's how."

"Whatever, dawg, you just trying to block a nigga."

"Go for what you know while I focus on gettin' this bread."

"Trust and believe I am."

Blaze gulped the last of his third Corona and said, "Well, I'm out...help yourself to the rest of the beer."

"Cool. See you tomorrow."

Blaze left for good, and Junior continued to eat his chicken fingers and drink Corona. Delilah stepped in a few minutes later wearing some tight-fitted stretch jeans and a white halter exposing her belly ring. Junior's jaw nearly dropped to the floor when he saw her.

She stood about five foot seven with a McDonald's French fries complexion, green eyes; and long, brunette hair that hung past her shoulders. Her curvaceous hips looked ready to bust out of her jeans.

"Hey, BJ, what's up?" Delilah asked.

"Huh?" Junior asked, still fixated on her ass.

She smiled and said, "What's going on, Ice Cold?"

"Come on, ma, you know better than that. It's BJ to you, fam, and I'm Ice Cold to all my adorning fans out there."

"Oh, excuse me, *Mr. Sensitive.*"

"It's just doesn't feel right when people close to me call me Ice Cold. It's like someone who's the same age as I am calling me sir."

"Can I call you sir? It sounds so dignified."

"Hell no."

"Whatever. So, is your brother alright?"

"What are you talking about?"

"You don't know, do you?"

"Know what?"

"His plane going to Chicago was almost hijacked this morning. Your brother saved the day by beating the terrorist half to death."

"Damn, I didn't know...I've been here all day. Shit, lemme call him."

Junior called Maurice's cell, but it went straight to voicemail. He decided to send him a text instead. *Just checkin' to see if you're ok bro. Call me when you get a chance.*

"He isn't answering, huh?" she asked.

"Nah, so I sent him a text," he replied. "I'm sure he's alright or else someone from the family would've called me by now."

"You're probably right. Did you finish the last track yet?"

"Almost...I'll put the finishing touches on it tomorrow morning."

"That's great. I can't wait for your album to drop."

"Mike said our track is gonna be on Hot 97 tomorrow."

"Get out! For real?!"

"Hell yeah, and the video is gonna be on MTV Jams next week."

Junior stood up, and Delilah rushed over to him and gave him a big hug before looking up at him. He briefly gazed into her eyes before passionately kissing her. She didn't resist him and reciprocated by nearly sticking her tongue down his throat.

He suddenly pulled away and said, "I thought you weren't feeling me, Delilah. Why the sudden change?"

"I wanted you from day one," she answered, "but I wasn't gonna play myself. I had to see what you were about first."

"I ain't mad at you, ma, but I didn't think I was your type...I mean...I thought you were kind of square."

"Square? What's that supposed to mean?"

"No disrespect, babe. I think you're hot to death, but you're so proper with your perfect diction and reading glasses and shit. You remind me of a Catholic schoolgirl."

"Don't you know that Catholic schoolgirls are the naughtiest freaks around?"

"Just how naughty is naughty?"

"Let's get out of here, and I'll show you how naughty I can be, BJ."

"You ain't said nothing but a word. Come on, we can go to my place. The view from my Manhattan apartment is off the chain."

"Lead the way, daddy."

# Chapter 6

I woke up on the couch with Maurice Jr. wrapped in my arms asleep. Jet lag had finally set in after our trip back home from the Virgin Islands and the trip to Chicago from St. Louis. I wasted no time crashing after playing with the children once I got back from Sean's place. Gabby and Gina had left out to catch a movie; and Rick was working on his next book in the room that he and Gina renovated into an office space in their five-bedroom home in Naperville, Illinois. Michael was also asleep on the other end of the couch, and Alexa was asleep in her crib in one of the guestrooms. I got up without waking Maurice Jr. and went to check on Alexa, and she was in the same position that I left her in before I took my nap. Jason was spending the night with a friend who stayed down the street from Rick and Gina's.

It was still daylight outside, but dusk was rapidly setting in. The window in the guestroom was slightly opened, and the crickets chirped steadily in their spacious backyard. I had turned my phone off because of the constant calls from reporters all afternoon—fifty-one voicemail messages and thirty-three text messages to be exact. Shit. I listened to ten of them before simply hanging up the phone. I then checked my texts and saw that I had one from Gabrielle, one from Junior, and one from Malik. Malik and Erin's plane had landed, and they were staying at Dad's. Junior was checking on me to see if I was okay, and Gabrielle's text read: *Heading over to Jasmine's for a little while. Will be back before midnight. Luv u.*

I smiled and placed my phone on the kitchen table before getting a beer out of the fridge. I then put the kids to bed and started flicking channels on television. Rick was on pace to burn the midnight oil, so I had to find my own entertainment. I finally settled on a baseball game before Gina walked in. She was every bit as beautiful as Gabrielle—five foot eight, a curvaceous body; and flawless, olive brown skin. Her ebony hair was long and silky, her lips were full and covered with ruby red lipstick, and she always commanded attention whenever she entered a room. She was forty years old, but she looked much younger—in fact, none of the women in Gabrielle's family looked their age. She placed her keys on a small living room table near the door and smiled at me.

"Hey, sis," I said.

"Hey, Maurice," she said. "You need anything?"

"Nah, I'm good. Didn't wanna tag along with Gabby over Jasmine's house, huh?"

"Nope, I just dropped her off and came home. They aren't my crowd...way too pretentious for my tastes. I don't even get down like that."

"I hear you...Stephanie's family hated me from jump street, too."

Gina walked toward the kitchen, and she turned around and said, "Can we talk?"

"Sure, is everything alright?"

"Oh yeah...nothing to worry about. I just need to say something to you."

We sat at the kitchen table after I grabbed another beer. She placed my hand in between her hands and said, "I want to apologize for the way I behaved when Gabby turned up missing...I've been dancing around the issue for three years now, and I feel there's still a little tension between us. I never got a chance to tell you how sorry I truly was, and you didn't deserve what we put you through. I hope you can forgive me someday."

"I already have, sis. I'm glad you are able to finally get this off of your chest so that you can move on. Life is too short to hold grudges, and nobody knows that better than me."

"Thank you," she said, leaning over to kiss me on the cheek. "I promise to keep it real with you from now on...."

"I understand why you did what you did," I interjected. "That fuckin' psychotic ex of hers was gonna kill her but ended up shooting me instead. Your loyalty was to your sister, and I can't be mad at you about that. I have to admit though...I wasn't gonna ever speak to you again, but nearly dying kind of changes your perspective on things."

"You're a good man, Maurice. I see why Gabby is so crazy about you."

"Thank you for the compliment."

I got up from my chair and gave Gina a hug before motioning back to the living room to watch the game. Rick came out of his study to take a break from writing while Gina warmed up some leftover dinner on the stove. Rick was the epitome of vanity—a six foot two inch, bodybuilding metrosexual with arched eyebrows and manicured hands. He let go of his regular job as a high school English teacher five years ago to pursue his dream as a writer and hasn't looked back since.

"I see you're up," Rick said, sitting down on the sofa. "Man, I heard you snoring even with the door closed."

"Shit, I was tired," I said. "If you had four kids, you'd know how I feel."

"And that's why I decided I didn't want to have them. Kids will make your ass old before your time, bro. Look at me, I look damn good for forty-five."

"No doubt you look good, but the reward of having kids is worth the sacrifice. So, how does Gina feel about not having kids?"

"Believe it or not, I wanted kids in the beginning of our marriage, but she didn't because she was trying to get established in her career. Now, our desires to have children have shifted...she wants to have a baby before she can't get pregnant anymore, and I'm simply not down with it. She calls me selfish, but truth be told, I'm enjoying life too much to be saddled with a baby."

"No room for compromise, huh?"

"And give up the freedom we have? Hell no, and besides, I'll be damn near collecting social security before the kid finishes high school."

I took a swig of my beer and said, "So, how's the next bestseller coming?"

"It's coming...having a little writer's block right now, and that's why I'm taking a break."

"What's it about?"

"It's a mystery detective thriller...an ex black ops agent goes rogue and is contracted to bump off some key people, and it's up to this detective to figure out his next move and save the day."

"I can't wait for it to drop...I'll be the first person in line to support you."

"I'll have the first copy autographed and signed just for you, brother-in-law."

Gina came in the living room with her plate and drink and sat down on the sofa in between Rick and me. She grabbed the remote and said, "Can we watch something else?"

"What, like the Food Network?" Rick asked in a sarcastic tone.

"I don't ever hear you complaining when you eat my cooking," Gina fired back.

"It's cool," I interjected, attempting to diffuse the potential argument before it got started. "I'm not really into this game anyway. Maybe we can watch a movie or something...I got a couple of them in my suitcase."

"That's a great idea," Gina said, looking in Rick's direction.

"Whatever Gina wants, Gina gets," Rick said sarcastically.

"You know what," Gina countered.

"Chill, y'all," I interjected. "It's not that deep."

"What's up with the bachelor party tonight?" Rick asked, changing the subject.

"I wouldn't call it a traditional bachelor party," I answered. "High society doesn't do things the way we do them."

"What, no strippers and booze?" Rick asked.

"No, silly," Gina chimed in. "The guys are watching the fight over at Brendan's."

"Sounds more like a damn funeral to me," Rick said. "How come you're not going, bro?"

"That's good to hear. I can't wait to make you Mrs. Moss."

"Stephanie Moss...that has a nice ring to it."

"Yes, it does."

There was a pause before Stephanie said, "So, are you sure that you and the fellas aren't going to hire some strippers to cap off the night? I'm the last woman you'll ever see naked, so I give you permission to get a lap dance or two."

"You are all the woman I'll ever need to see naked from this point on...besides, neither my family or yours would ever approve of such behavior. A blemish to the family name like partying with strippers the night before my wedding might warrant being disowned completely."

"I guess you have a point, but haven't you ever wanted to just cut loose?"

"Yes, and I have, but I've gotten all of that foolishness out of my system."

"Well, okay then, my love. I have no problem with you being on your best behavior. What do you all have going on besides watching the fight?"

"Nothing much...we have hot wings, beer and a deck of cards."

"That's great. I hope you guys enjoy yourselves, and try not to drink too much. I love you, baby."

"I love you, too. Bye."

"Bye."

Brendan smiled as he placed his phone on the dresser. Ricardo entered his closet a few seconds later.

"Looking real dapper, little brother," Ricardo said. "Are you ready?"

"Yeah, I good," Brendan replied. "I knew I was going to marry her the first time I saw her. She's the one."

"I agree...she is the one. Don't fuck it up, bro."

"I won't, man, I promise you that. I finally got my life on track, and I'm ready to take things to the next level."

"That's good to know...learn from my mistakes, Brendan. I lived life on the edge, and it cost me. Now I've got a five-figure alimony and child support payment every month for the next fifteen years."

"I have...and believe it or not I still look up to you, Ricky. You're the reason I got into the financial industry...not dad, and not mom."

"I'm flattered, but how good is life for you in the financial industry? Last time I checked, the economy was in pretty bad shape."

"Life is good because I don't take unnecessary risks. I've become a major player by doing things the right way."

"I hope so...."

"You hope so? What does that mean, Ricky?"

"Marcus Doss...how well do you trust him?"

"He's my frat brother...I trust him completely."

"How many times have I told you that you can completely trust anyone in this game? You all are entrusted to billions of dollars of other people's money. One false move, and you could do serious time."

"What are you talking about? Marc is my business partner, and we always do things by the book."

"All I'm saying is watch your back. Hire an accountant and a lawyer to keep an eye on him...trust and believe he's hired one of each to watch you."

"Huh? We're not Bernie Madoff, or anybody like him."

"I'm just trying to look out for you, bro."

"I appreciate it, but don't spoil my night, okay?"

"Okay. So, is Stephanie's ex Ousley still giving you a hard time?"

"Nah, we're cool. He was just looking out for her...you know, she's like family to them."

"That shit doesn't make you even a little jealous?"

"It's not like that. Maurice is crazy about his wife...and Stephanie is good friends with both of them."

"If you say so...seems a little strange to me...."

"I'm good, man, don't you have any faith in me?"

"Yeah, just don't stick your head in the sand when it comes to them. You're the outsider in their little inner circle, so keep your eyes open."

"You know, you're way too judgmental of people...."

"Food for thought, little brother. Come on, the rest of the fellas are starting to roll in for the fight."

# Chapter 8

Junior sat on his bed eagerly anticipating what Delilah was going to look like once she came out of the bathroom from freshening up. He had tried to set the mood by lighting some candles and pouring them two glasses of Moscato that he placed on his dresser. He wasn't much of a wine drinker, but he knew that girls liked it.

He put a Trey Songz CD in to further set the mood right, and Delilah came out of the bathroom wearing nothing but her black silk underwear and her stilettos. She had put on a touch of makeup and some lip gloss to accentuate her full, sensuous lips. Delilah Sosa had a Dominican heritage but was born and bred in New York City. She spoke fluid Spanish and English, and all she ever wanted to do in life was be an entertainer.

Her sexy bosom and derriere made Junior's eyes bulge and mouth gape open in astonishment. She walked over to the bed and grabbed his hand as he stood up to gaze into her eyes.

"You are so damn beautiful," he whispered.

"Shhh," she said. "Take off your shirt, baby."

He did exactly what he was told and took off his t-shirt before tossing it on the floor. She then slowly began to rub his muscular chest and arms—digging her French-tip nails lightly into his back afterwards. He pulled her closer to him and kissed the side of her neck, then he planted light pecks on her left cheek, and then he finally tasted her sweet lips. She could feel the throbbing bulge in his pants as they passionately kissed for a moment before collapsing onto the bed.

He took the lead by unfastening her bra while burying his face into her chest. The dulcet smell of her perfume had ignited his unadulterated passion as he worked his way down her stomach to her pleasure cove after removing her panties. She squirmed from the almost unbearable pleasure he gave her—belting out a harmonious squeal seconds before her first climax.

Delilah then aggressively turned Junior over on his back and started kissing his smooth, golden-brown skin—beginning with his left ear. She licked his inner ear and lightly blew her hot, sweet breath inside of it. He was instantly aroused, and he moaned in ecstasy and became fully erected. She wasted no time working her way down to his soldier standing at full attention once she saw how much he was into her.

She too, became completely aroused after indulging herself in pleasuring him to the fullest. They worked each other over repeated with wickedly pulsating thrusts and grinds—their only thoughts were to simply pleasure each other in every way humanly possible. They made love until they both had nothing left to give—exploring every inch of each other's body leaving no stone unturned. Their bond was forged—months of uncontrollable desire and passion had been uncorked.

They held one another once they were done—each wondering what the other was thinking. Was this only a one-night stand? Or should we try out being a couple? He finally broke the silence by saying, "So, what does the future hold for us? I hope I'm not playing myself when I say that I'm really into you. I've only been in a commitment relationship once, but she kicked me to the curb. I wanna take a chance with you, but I don't know...."

"I want the same thing you do, BJ, but I'm afraid, too. I don't know how we make this work because I don't want the public all in our business. We might not make it if that happens."

He kissed her softly and said, "I agree with you, but I'm willing to take that chance. I think you're worth it."

"I think you're worth it, too, but I'm not ready to be open about it yet. Let's just keep it on the DL and enjoy getting to know one another first."

"Okay, I like the sound of that. Besides, we need to focus on our music right now anyway."

"Absolutely. So, who's the girl who broke your heart?"

"Nobody. We were in two different places in our lives, and we were basically doomed from the start."

"Nobody, huh? What's her name?"

"Her name is Tamara...Tamara White. We went to college together for a year before she graduated and moved on."

"*The* Tamara White on Hot 97?"

"Yeah, *that* Tamara...I'm sure I'mma have to go to the radio station soon to promote the album. I just hope the interview won't be with her."

"Damn, that's crazy. Well, don't worry about it. I'm sure everything will work itself out."

"You're so cool, Delilah, and just so you know, you don't have to worry about Tamara. I'm over her."

"I aim to please, baby, and thanks for telling me about her. I trust you."

He leaned in for another kiss and said, "I trust you, too."

# Chapter 9

I was working on my fourth Corona while shooting the breeze with Rick and Gina before Malik and my sister Erin stopped by. A small family get-together turned out to be a mini party because Malik bought more food and drink, and Gabrielle and her two sorority sisters Ciera and Brittany arrived moments after Malik and Erin did.

Erin hugged me and said, "I'm so thankful that you two are still alive. What were you thinking, Maurice? Do you have a death wish?"

"We wouldn't be standing here and talking to you right now if I didn't do something Erin," I answered.

"It always has to be you, doesn't it?" she asked.

"Forget about what she's saying, bro," Malik said, looking at my swollen hand. "I'm proud of you, man...that terrorist didn't stand a chance."

"Thanks, man, I appreciate that," I said.

"Walk with me over here," Malik said.

I gulped the last of my beer and followed Malik to a corner of the living room for some privacy. I wanted another beer, but I knew if I drank much more, I'd be going to Stephanie's wedding with a hangover. I liked to drink quite frequently since retirement, but I always monitored my intake because I hated paying for overindulging in life's sinful pleasures. I liked the feeling of being buzzed, but I hated being drunk. Could I possibly have a drinking problem? Maybe. I always had control over my drinking except that summer when Gabrielle disappeared a

"Maurice?" she asked, obviously baffled. "What are you doing here?"

"I should ask you the same question. The text that Marc was supposed to get came to me. So, what gives?"

"I rather not say...I guess you were on my mind after what happened today. Are you okay?"

"I'm fine, Steph, thanks for asking, but don't try to change the subject. What's going on?"

"You wouldn't understand...."

"Try me...I didn't drive all the way down here just to turn back around. You better tell me something."

"Alright...I don't know if I can go through with this...."

"Go through with what, the wedding?"

"Yes, Maurice, the wedding."

"Why, and what does this have to do with Brendan's business partner, Marc?"

"Marc and I...we've been sneaking around with each other for the past six months, and I came here tonight to break it off with him."

"What the fuck, Steph?! What are you doing? Are you crazy?"

"First of all, you really need to calm down. This is none of your damn business."

"Wrong, you made it my business when you sent me that text. What happened to you, baby? You are not acting like the Stephanie I know. The whole time I thought my antennas were telling me that Brendan was shady, but it turns out you're the one who being unfaithful."

"FYI, I'm not the Stephanie you once knew. Yes, I'm the shady one, but don't you dare judge me with your self-righteous bullshit."

"Self-righteous bullshit? I'm not judging you...lord knows I'm not perfect, but I simply don't understand this. Brendan is a great guy, so why are you cheating on him? Shit, you're a damn good actress because I could've sworn you were happy."

"Yes, Brendan is a great guy, and I was happy at first, but I don't love him. Believe me, I tried to love him, but the sparks just aren't there."

"So what, you love Marc?"

"Hell no. Marc ain't shit...what we had was strictly sexual."

"Then what's the fuckin' problem? Love isn't something you try to do...it's either there or it isn't."

"Exactly. I don't love Brendan because he ain't you, Maurice. I'm still in love with you."

"Huh? We've been through this Steph...I love Gabrielle and only Gabrielle. You can't marry this dude because you aren't being fair to him or yourself."

"What the fuck am I supposed to do, Maurice? I want to be happy, too...I'll learn to love Brendan in time."

"You do what you think is best Steph, but what you're doing right now is fucked up. Sleeping with that no-good motherfucker Marc is foul."

"Fuck you, Maurice."

"Whatever...do what you want to do. I'm out."

"Don't say shit to anybody...I'll handle this my way."

"Well, it's like you said, it's none of my damn business, right?" I asked with sarcasm, and I left.

# Chapter 10

Darius had just finished packing a bag and was going to catch the first Greyhound to New York as soon as possible. He had time to think about the option Agent Greenwood had given him, but he decided to put yet another town in his rearview mirror instead. His mission was to find his friend Donnie Lucas and warn him about what was about to go down in the next day or so, and he planned on disappearing afterwards forever. Relocating to Toronto, Canada seemed like a great place to start; and in his mind, the States had nothing else to offer him. I've should have done this a long time ago, he thought.

There was no way anyone was going to believe that he didn't shoot Ousley, and he didn't have the energy or the resources to even try to prove his innocence. Besides, he was already wanted for violating his parole, extortion, and the murder of Chandler. One thing was certain; he wasn't about to become a snitch under any circumstances even though his cousin Mike betrayed him. He even thought about taking him out, but he couldn't wrap his mind around killing his own flesh and blood. At any rate, Mike was dead to him anyway.

He pondered how he was going to find Donnie because he hadn't used a cellphone since fleeing LA, and he knew Donnie was now flagged by the Feds just like he was. He remembered some of the clubs Donnie frequented, and he was going to start by tracking him down at one of his favorite spots in Harlem, Billie's Black Bar Lounge.

He proceeded to grab his bag after making sure he had his wallet and passport when he heard a knock at the door. He panicked because he thought it was Greenwood, and his first thought was to run out the back door of his apartment. However, his instincts told him to open the front door and deal with whoever was behind it.

"You were just gonna leave without saying goodbye, huh?" Megan asked angrily, noticing his packed bag on the floor. "You never came back after talking to that strange guy."

"Megan, what are you doing here?" Darius asked. "There's so much that you don't know about me. Trust me, it's better this way."

"I'm here because I was concerned about you...."

"Don't worry about me, sweetie. I'm the one your mother warned you about. I suggest that you do yourself a favor and forget about me...."

"I couldn't forget about you even if I wanted to. I've been trying to let you know how I feel about since the first time I saw you, but you never look my way."

"I'm no good, Megan. The last thing I want to do is fuck up your life. I think you're a nice girl, but I can't go there with you."

"Why? What are you afraid of, Darren? I won't hurt you...."

"Darius...my real name is Darius, and I'm not afraid. It's just that...I...look, I gotta go. It was nice knowing you."

"Baby, wait."

Megan pulled Darius close and locked lips with his. He reluctantly pulled away a few seconds later and said, "I can't do this...."

"You felt something just like I did," she said. "I don't care about your past, sweetheart. All that's important is the here and now."

Even though Darius came off as a quiet and unassuming person, the very essence of him exuded a power and a presence that drew her in instantly. He unknowingly cast a spell on her that she couldn't shake. Now, it was her turn to cast her spell on him. He hadn't been with a woman in over thirteen years, and it was impossible for him to resist her sexiness any longer.

He picked her up, and she wrapped her legs around his waist as he carted her off to his bedroom. He was inebriated by her kisses that seemed to go on and on indefinitely. Neither of them wanted to stop as blood money that came with a price. Her doorbell rang before she could take a sip of her tequila.

"Who is it?" she asked.

"It's Blaze," he answered.

She opened the door in disgust as he walked past her. Blaze was the reason she came back across the border because they started a relationship not long after Terrence was murdered, and they both felt comforting each other was a good idea at the time. However, his philandering ways had worn thin on her.

"What the fuck do you want, Blaze?" she said angrily.

"I just wanted to see you, baby," he answered. "I miss you...I miss us."

"I'm not falling for your bullshit anymore. I am *so* over you."

"I said I was sorry, Sally. I'll never cheat on you again. Just give us another chance."

"Sorry, sweetheart, I can't do that. Opening my heart to you was a big ass mistake...Terry would be so disappointed in me."

"What the fuck...Terrence is gone and he's never coming back. You need to let that shit go and stop feeling guilty about moving on."

"You just don't get it, do you?"

"Get what? He would have wanted you to be happy...."

"That's just it...I'm not happy with you. What I had with Terry was real, and I took a gigantic step backwards fuckin' with your sorry ass."

"Man, that's some fucked up shit to say, Sally."

"No, it's the goddamn truth, Simon."

"Well, can I at least see Kevin?"

"He ain't here. He ran outta here a few minutes ago."

"Do you know where he went?"

"No, but if you find him, tell him not to come back here tonight. I'm tired of his ungrateful ass, too. I have my son to look after, and I don't have time for his bullshit either."

"So, you're gonna give up on my little man, too?"

"If you care so much, you raise him because I'm done."

"Fine, he can live with me then. We're all he's got...you really need to check yourself, Sally."

"Why don't you go fuck one of your groupie hoes?"

"I'm not gonna let you keep dissin' me...."

"Just get the fuck outta my house, Simon!"

"Fine, I'll leave, but I'm not giving up on us...."

"There is no *us*...there never was. You were there when I needed someone, but that's as far as it goes. I knew you were temporary the moment I let you in my life. You're not the settling-down type."

"I can be if you just give me another chance. Why don't you make our house a home, baby? Make an honest man outta me."

"No, Simon, just leave, please...."

"I love you, Sally," he pleaded.

"I don't love you, Simon," she said holding the door open for him. "Goodbye."

Blaze left feeling rejected and dejected. He realized that their relationship was over, and all he wanted to do was get high—real high. He then decided to go to the dope spot to get a bag to smoke away his problems.

# Chapter 12

I got back to my in-laws still seething from my encounter with Stephanie. I realized on the drive back that nothing with her had really changed—she had just become a master at hiding her true self, that's all. I was more mad at myself for allowing her back in my life, and I felt Gabrielle needed to know the truth about her once and for all.

I wasn't mad at the fact that she still had feelings for me because a part of me would always love her, too, but I was mad because she pretended to be Gabrielle's friend and pretended to be sprung on a man she didn't love. I didn't like phony people around me, and I wasn't going to give Stephanie a pass just because we had history together.

I went inside and tossed Rick's keys on a coffee table in living room area. Gabrielle was talking to one of her soros when she noticed that I was back. She had sensed that something was going on with me and walked over to comfort me. I grabbed her hand and kissed it.

"Are you okay, baby?" she asked, gently stroking my back.

"No, Gabby," I answered, "let's go outside and talk."

We stepped outside on the front porch, and I shut the door behind us. She looked into my eyes and grabbed both of my hands.

"What did you do, get lost?" she asked. "You were gone forever."

"Nah, nothing like that," I answered solemnly. "I lied to you, and I'm sorry."

"Lied about what, Maurice?"

"I didn't go to the liquor store...Stephanie had sent me a text, and I met her at the South Loop Club."

"Huh? What the fuck is going on?"

"It's not what you think."

"Then, what I'm I supposed to think?"

"The text I got from her wasn't meant for me...she sent me a text thinking she had sent the text to Marc."

"She sent you a text that was meant for Marc? Why the hell is she texting Marc?"

"They are having an affair, and she was going to break it off with him tonight."

"The night before her wedding...damn, that's fucked up on so many levels. And she didn't even let me know what was going on with her."

"That's not even the best part. She tells me that she never loved Brendan, and that she messed around with Marc for the sex. Imagine that."

"Unbelievable. You think you know a person, and then boom, they turn around and do something crazy like this. Wait until I talk to her ass tomorrow."

"Hell-no, Gabby, we're catching the first thing moving tomorrow morning. Fuck Stephanie and fuck her goddamn wedding."

"Wait, baby, I can't leave my girl hanging like that...why are you tripping?"

"How are you going to be able to look Brendan in the face knowing what you know?"

"What she did doesn't have anything to do with you or me."

"No, that's where you're wrong...I didn't tell you the kicker. Stephanie is not your friend or your sister. She's pretending to be your friend because she's still in love with me."

"What?! You've got to be kidding me."

"I wish I was...but I heard it right out of the horse's mouth tonight. As of now, I'm done with her. I don't like fake-ass people around me."

"Wow, I can't believe her," she said, pausing for a brief moment.

"I can't believe her, either, and I don't want to be anywhere near Brendan's house tomorrow."

"Did she try to kiss you?" she said, raising an eyebrow.

"No, it was like that," I answered, trying to reassure her. "She was just making an affirmation about how she truly felt."

"Oh, okay. Deep down, I've always known she wasn't over you, but I also know she would never act on those feelings."

"And how do you know that?"

"It's a woman thing. She didn't ask you to leave me and the kids, did she?"

"No, she didn't. She basically told me that I was self-righteous and to go fuck myself."

"You see, just because a woman tells a man that she loves him, it doesn't mean she wants to be with him. She already knows that you're committed to me and our family, and she also knows that it wouldn't work between the two of you."

"Why are you being Mother Teresa and shit? I just knew you were going to want to beat her ass."

"Why? She didn't do anything. She's trying to move on with her life the best way she can. If she still wants to marry Brendan, I'll stand by her side."

"Are you crazy, Gabby? So, you saying that you still want to be her friend after all this?"

"No, that's not what I'm saying...I'm going to honor my commitment to her. After that, we will distance ourselves from them."

"Okay, I can live with that."

"I agree that spending so much time with them isn't a healthy situation, but sometimes you have to keep your enemies closer."

"You were pretending to like Steph just so you could keep an eye on her, huh?"

"No, I wasn't pretending...I *do* love Stephanie, but I'm not blind. I had my suspicions about her just like you had suspicions about Brendan. After tomorrow, we can cut our ties to them for good."

"Good, I'm glad we agree on this. Let's enjoy the rest of the party."

# Chapter 13

Blaze had copped a bag of *kush* from a dealer he knew in Harlem with his boys Peanut and Bam. He picked them up from his place after his argument with Sally, and they planned on getting high before heading over to the studio. He promised them that they were going to be on one of his tracks for the album, and he flew them out to New York from LA for the weekend. Peanut and Bam weren't under contract with the label, so Blaze was going to pay them out of his own pocket.

Blaze pulled up in the lot of the studio while Bam rolled the blunts in the backseat. Blaze noticed that Sally's nephew was standing by the entrance of the studio when he parked his car.

"That looks like Kevin over there," Peanut said.

"Yeah, that is my little man," Blaze said. "Hold up, y'all better not start without me."

Blaze got out of the car and walked toward Kevin. He stood waiting patiently with his hands in his pockets.

"Yo, little man, what you doin' here?" Blaze asked.

"I got into it with auntie, Blaze," Kevin replied. "She's always in my shit...I had to get outta there. She found my stash."

"I know...I was just by there. She's mad at me too."

"I can't stay there anymore...she's got all these rules and shit...."

"She's just tryin' to do what's best for you, little man."

"You sound just like her, man. Fuck it, I shouldn't have come here...."

"Wait...."

"What?"

"You can stay with me."

"Word?"

"Yeah, come on. We're about to smoke a bag in the car before we head up the studio. If your skills are on point, I'll let you be on the track."

"Hell yeah, my skills are *way* on point."

They walked back over to the car, and Peanut and Bam had already started the rotation. Bam passed Blaze the Blunt and said, "We tried to wait on you, but y'all were takin' too fuckin' long. What up, little man?"

"It's all good, Bam," Kevin said. "When y'all get here?"

"We flew in last night," Bam answered. "Wanna hit this?"

Kevin looked at Blaze for his approval, and Blaze nodded and said, "Go ahead, my nigga, you're smokin' that shit already anyway."

Kevin took a puff and passed it to Peanut. Peanut then took a puff and said, "Sorry about your great-grandmother, little man. She was like my grandmother too. She looked out for everybody on the block, homeboy."

"Thanks, Nut," Kevin said. "I'm cool, though. I'm taking it like a man."

"That's what I'm talkin' 'bout, lil' nigga," Bam added. "Take that shit like a real G."

Blaze took another puff and said, "Little man is gonna be on the track, too. He says he can spit, so we're gonna see if his vocals are up to par."

"That's what's up," Peanut said. "We're gonna see what you got."

"Yeah, little man," Bam said, "this track is gonna be off the chain."

They all continued to get high for about thirty minutes more before going inside of the studio. It was already passed midnight, and nobody else was there. Blaze was going to have to play the engineer and lay down his vocals later.

Mike Clinton only had three signed artists—Blaze, Junior and

Delilah. Mike's first act was a rapper who left him for a bigger label because he didn't have him under contract, and he dropped his next artist before signing Blaze and Junior because the album bombed and didn't net him a profit. Delilah was there with him from the beginning, and her loyalty to the label was about to pay off. He had everything riding on them, and if things didn't work out, the label was destined to fold.

Meanwhile, Junior had just dropped Delilah off to pick up her car, and he planned on going up to the studio afterwards to get the reminder of the beer out of the fridge.

"I had a great time tonight," Delilah said. "I hope we can create many more wonderful memories."

"I had a great time, too," Junior said. "As for creating many more wonderful memories, I'm all for that."

She leaned toward him, and they passionately kissed for a few minutes or so. They finally pulled away from each other, and Junior said, "I'll call you tomorrow after I finish this last track."

"Okay," she said. "What do you have going on later?"

"I don't know...what do you wanna do?"

"I want an encore, baby."

"You got it."

He kissed her goodbye, and she drove off moments later. He then went inside of the studio and found the guys rehearsing.

"It's about time you got to work, homie," Junior said, giving Blaze dap. "These are your homeboys?"

"Yeah," Blaze answered, "this is Bam, and this is Peanut. And that's Kevin on the mic."

"Nice to meet y'all," Junior said, shaking both of their hands.

"Yo, you're nice on the mic, homie," Bam said.

"Yeah, you got mad skills, man," Peanut added.

"Thanks, fellas," Junior said, appreciatively. "Yo, little man got skills, too."

"Yeah, he's tight," Blaze said. "He's gonna be on one of my tracks with these guys."

"That's hot, Blaze," Junior said, grabbing a beer out of the fridge.

"Yo, pass me one, too," Blaze said.

"Y'all want one?" Junior asked.

"Nah, I'm good," Peanut answered. "I'm on next."

"I'm good, too," Bam answered. "I'm on last."

"We can get some more a little later," Blaze added. "I like the vibe in here, so it shouldn't take too long to finish this track."

They wrapped up the song about an hour and a half later, and then it was off to the liquor store. Blaze was going to add his sixteen bars later on that day and have the sound engineer mix the track afterwards.

They ended up going back to Blaze's place with the beer, and they planned on drinking and playing Madden NFL 12. They were all bragging the entire ride about who was going to take all the money from the bet. Since there were five of them, they flipped coins to see who was going to get the bye, and the other four were going to square off against each other. The rule was the person who won by the biggest margin got to sit out until the final game while the other winner played the person with the bye.

This competition continued until the wee hours of the morning, and all of them were drunk and talking shit by then. Junior was disgusted at the fact that Blaze had allowed Kevin to drink but held his tongue—he was very cognizant of the fact that one false move could land him back in prison for a long time. Kevin had won the bet and was talking the most trash out of everyone. He couldn't hold his liquor too well at thirteen years old, and he was well beyond being out of control.

"Sit your ass down, lil' nigga," Bam shouted, "before I fuck you up."

"Shut the fuck up, Bam," Kevin countered. "You ain't gonna do shit, muthafucka."

"Slow your role, little man," Blaze warned. "This is a grown-ass man you're talking to."

"Aw, fuck him," Kevin said. "His short ass ain't fadin' nothin' over here. He ain't even six feet tall and shit."

"You need to get your man, Blaze," Junior warned. "He's gonna get his ass killed."

"Yeah, Blaze," Peanut added. "Calm his young ass down."

"Chill the fuck out, little man," Blaze said. "You're being real disrespectful right now."

"Fuck-all-y'all!" Kevin shouted. "Bam's just mad 'cus I beat his ass in the finals."

Bam stood up to punch Kevin in the face, but Peanut grabbed him and said, "Nah, Bam, you can't go out like that. You already got two strikes, *damu*."

"You need to shut your ass up, Kevin," Junior said, "before my man lights you up. Just take that money and sit your ass down."

"Who the fuck are you, bitch?" Kevin asked. "You the only one in here who ain't down. I'll blast your ass, you mark-ass busta!"

"You got me fucked up, lil' homie," Junior answered as he stood up from the couch. "I'm from the streets too, now what?!"

"Fuck you, you fake rappin' muckafucka!" Kevin yelled. "You ain't from the streets, fraud-ass nigga!"

"Don't ever question my gangsta, yungin'!" Junior yelled back. "Don't make me put my hands on you!"

Blaze hauled off and snacked Kevin in the face and said, "If you don't shut the fuck up, I'm gonna beat your ass myself!"

"He obviously can't hold his liquor, Blaze," Junior said. "Don't give his ass shit else."

"You suck, *Ice Cold*," Kevin said. "Don't nobody even believe that shit you be rappin' about...my man right here blasted your brother, and you never even tried to find out who did it...."

"What you say, muthafucka?" Junior asked curtly.

"I didn't stutter," Kevin answered. "Bam shot your brother three years ago in LA. He was on some prove-your-loyalty shit when he shot him at that gas station. He got mad pub 'cus your brother was a big-time celebrity unlike your fake ass. It was business, nothing personal."

Junior glared at Bam, and then he turned his attention to Blaze and said, "Is that true, Blaze? Did Bam shoot my brother?"

"I don't know," Blaze answered. "I was too busy burying my man when that shit happened...I was done with the street life by then. Did you shoot 'um, Bam?"

Bam stood up and said, "Yeah, I shot him, *damu*, and that dude from New York is America's Most Wanted because of it."

He then turned his attention to Junior and said, "What the fuck you gonna do about it, cuz?"

"I'm gonna fuckin' kill you!" Junior shouted.

Bam rushed Junior and swung on him, but Junior ducked and punched him dead in the face. Peanut tried to swing on him, but Junior decked him and knocked him out cold with one punch—his father Brent Sr. had taught him well. He proceeded to pound Bam's face repeatedly with such force that it was blood everywhere. Blaze finally pulled Junior off of him and locked his arms around him.

"Calm the fuck down, BJ!" Blaze said. "I swear I didn't know, man! I had nothing to do with that shit. I had just gotten out of jail, and I was focusing on trying to stay out."

"Let me go!" Junior said. "You mean to tell me your so-called friends knew about this shit and you didn't? That's bullshit!"

"I swear on my mama I didn't know!" Blaze shouted. "Look what the fuck you done, Kevin!"

"I'm sorry, Blaze," Kevin said, "I didn't want it to go down like this...."

"What the fuck do mean you didn't want it to go down like this?!" Blaze asked tersely. "You instigated this whole shit! Get the fuck outta here and go home! Now!"

Kevin quickly left the apartment, and Blaze went over to check Bam's pulse before Peanut woke up. Peanut then slowly stood up, looked at Junior, and then turned his attention to Blaze and Bam.

"Call 911, Nut," Blaze said. "He ain't breathing."

"I'm gonna kill you if my man doesn't make it," Peanut said angrily, looking directly at Junior.

"I'm right here," Junior said, raising both of his arms in the air.

"Both of y'all chill the fuck out!" Blaze shouted. "Hurry up, Nut, he's still ain't breathing!"

Peanut called 911, and Blaze continued to give Bam CPR. Blaze did manage to revive Bam, but his pulse was very weak. The paramedics arrived about ten minutes later, and they worked on him for several minutes more before taking him to the hospital. Thc three of them trailed the ambulance in Blaze's car.

"Damn, my man is fucked up in there," Peanut said. "He's gotta make it."

"He's gonna make it, Nut," Blaze said. "The whole situation is fucked up. This is all Kevin's fault."

"No disrespect, Blaze," Junior said after having time to sober up, calm down and think, "but you can't put this all on him. The truth always comes out, and in the end, nobody gets away with the dirt they do."

"Who the fuck asked you?" Peanut asked, turning his head and directing his comment to Junior sitting in the back seat. "This shit is all your fault!"

"Nah, Nut," Blaze added. "I would've reacted the same way if somebody told me they shot my brother. You can't blame him...."

"There's plenty of blame to go around," Junior injected, "and I'm truly sorry about what went down. What happened tonight was fate...this was destined to happen, and I will accept my punishment if he doesn't make it."

They rode in silence the remainder of the trip to the hospital after Junior's comment. Junior replayed the events over and over in his head and realized that he wouldn't have—he couldn't have done anything differently. He had prayed for Bam to pull through in spite of the circumstances, but he was fully prepared for the worst possible outcome—being sent to prison for the rest of his life.

# Chapter 14

Darius came off of Interstate 64 somewhere near Lexington, KY to get some gas; and Megan was sound asleep on the passenger's side. They had been on the highway for roughly five hours, and daylight was moments away. Megan had a 1994 Honda Accord that was hell on gas—they hadn't even driven 300 miles before the first fill up. Darius was leery of stopping anywhere for fear of being recognized on a Crime Stoppers billboard or FBI Most Wanted poster. It had gotten to the point that he was extremely paranoid whenever he was in public for a long period of time, and he had become reclusive because of it.

He once saw himself on a Crime Stoppers billboard shortly after fleeing Los Angeles; and his electronic image was plastered across a fifty-foot high sign right outside of Santa Fe, New Mexico while he was eating lunch at a local restaurant. A cold chill permeated his body once he saw himself on display, but luckily no one had recognized him. He immediately left the restaurant after paying the waitress and didn't finish his food.

He pulled alongside pump seven and got out to pay the clerk inside the gas station. Megan had awakened from her sleep and got out herself to use the restroom. He bought a Mountain Dew and paid the clerk fifty dollars to fill up. There was nothing out of the ordinary during their brief pit stop until local law enforcement drove up. Megan had just bought some snack food after using the restroom and was on her way back to the car. The cop appeared to be running the license plate of Megan's car, and Darius nervously continued to pump the gas while trying to remain calm. Megan was oblivious to the cop parked a few yards behind them and plopped into the front passenger's seat. Darius never made direct eye contact with the cop and slowly drove off after he was finished. He couldn't put the whole fifty dollars worth of gas in the tank and left without receiving his change back.

"That's was a close call," Darius said.

"What was a close call, baby?" Megan asked.

"I think that cop was running your plates back there."

"Why? I'm clean."

"I'm not exactly sure, but seeing you with me probably didn't help much."

"You don't know that for sure...*it* is 2012...."

"And the world still hasn't changed much."

"You really need to let that go."

"Or maybe he recognized my face from an FBI Most Wanted poster or something."

Megan paused and then said, "Want me take over? I got enough sleep."

"Nah, that's okay... I got this Mountain Dew to keep me awake."

"Okay."

He continued to drive for about twenty miles before a speeding car rushed up behind them and rode his bumper briefly before turning on his red and blue flashing lights. He pulled over to the shoulder and parked, and then he pounded his fist on the dashboard in frustration.

"Fuck!" he shouted. "I knew that redneck motherfucker was gonna stop us."

"Just relax, baby," she said. "We didn't do anything wrong."

"You don't understand, Megan. Why do you think I've been running for the last three years?"

"You have an alias, don't you? That cop didn't recognize you or else he wouldn't have let us leave the lot."

"I'm wanted for murder and attempted murder, babe. That damn clerk probably saw my face somewhere...."

"Murder and attempted murder?"

"Yes, but I didn't exactly do either crime...."

The cop walked up the driver's side window and said, "License and registration, sir."

Darius handed the cop his driver's license and Megan's registration card. The cop looked it over and walked back to his patrol car.

"I'm fucked," Darius said. "This is probably the end of the road for me. I've tried to redeem myself by straightening out my life, but that's clearly not enough."

"Don't worry, everything will be alright. You said you didn't murder anybody, right?"

"Do you remember when that pro basketball player got shot at a gas station in LA a few years ago?"

"Uh...wasn't his name Maurice Ousley?"

"Yeah, I'm wanted for shooting him, but I didn't do it. I did try to extort money from him so that I could start my record label because his fiancee owed me money, but he tried to set me up with the Feds. He got shot the day after, and everyone thinks I did it."

"I see. You wanted him to pay her debt, but he wasn't going for it."

"Yeah, with interest, but once I sensed I was walking into a trap, I skipped town."

"How did you know his fiancee?"

"She was my ex."

"Wow, that's crazy...it's funny how life goes. You were smart for leaving town."

The cop walked back to the car and handed Darius his license and registration card back and said, "Be sure to get your left brake light fixed. Have a good day."

"Yes, sir," Darius said.

Darius slowly drove off after wiping the sweat off of his brow. He then maintained his speed at sixty-five and didn't go a mile over it.

"What the fuck was that all about?" Darius asked rhetorically.

"I don't know," Megan said. "Nobody gets stopped for a faulty brake light."

"Wait, I didn't get my change for the gas...I panicked when I saw the cop and just drove off. I had about ten dollars worth of change coming back because the tank was full, and the clerk probably said something to him."

"You're probably right about that. Hopefully, nothing like this will ever happen again."

"Yeah, hopefully not. I would've shot his ass in my former life...I guess I *have* changed."

"My instincts tell me that you're a good man."

"I'm not so sure...the verdict is still out on that."

"I can see that you're a changed man in the few months I've known you. The Darren I know would intently hurt anybody."

"You see all of that in me? I've done serious time, and I'd still be locked up if it wasn't for numerous appeals and diligence on my part."

"It just goes to show you anything is possible...you're living proof that anybody can change for the better. So, what made you change?"

"I really can't put a finger on it...I guess it was the small-town lifestyle. I was used to the hustle and bustle of New York, but the slower pace of Sikeston calmed me down. I hated it at first, but I've learned to appreciate the quietness over time."

"I'm from Omaha, Nebraska...not exactly a small town, but it's nothing compared to New York City."

"How did you end up in Sikeston?"

"I went to Southern Illinois University for a couple of years before I got send to prison, and I decided to come back to the area once I got out since I no longer had family to count on."

There was brief silence, and then Megan lit a cigarette. She took a puff and blew some smoke out of her nostrils.

"You said you're wanted for murder?" she asked, changing the subject.

"Yes, I am. I shot a guy in a drug deal gone bad at a warehouse in East LA the day before I skipped town, and my partner finished him off. The guy was bad news...he killed three other guys...two cops and a bodyguard before we put him down."

"I don't follow you exactly...were the cops trying to bust up your deal, and the guy you shot killed them?"

"No, it wasn't like that. The cops were dirty...my partner and I were going to make a buy from them, but this other guy ruined the deal. He had a beef with the dirty cops and had a score to settle with them."

"So, you got caught in the middle...your friend killed him because he was an obstacle in the way."

"I guess you can say that...I regretted ever going out there that night. The money and the drugs helped start the record label that my cousin is now running, though."

"What's the name of your record label?"

"It's called Rhymes and Lyrics Records."

"Damn, money shouldn't be a problem for you...I'm sure your cousin gives you your take, doesn't he?"

"I haven't seen a dime from that label...the Feds had flipped my cousin, and that's why I got a visit from the guy at the bar. He wanted me to set up a drug deal with my cousin and my partner in crime Donnie Lucas from the warehouse murders in East LA. Donnie's now the biggest drug dealer in New York, and the Feds want to take him down."

"You lived an interesting life, but none of that matters. I want us to start a new life together...let's just forget about New York and go straight to Canada."

"I wish I could, but I have to warn my friend. He needs to know who he's dealing with...my cousin Mike is going to bring him down, and I have to do something about it."

"You're too loyal for your own good. Promise me that all you're gonna do is warn him...please don't get involved in his shit. He chose the life he leads, and it's really not your responsibility to save him."

"All I'm gonna do is give him the heads up, that's all."

She kissed him on the cheek and whispered in his ear, "Good, because I think I'm falling in love with you."

"Not so fast, Megan, you barely know me," he said, grabbing her hand. "I'm no angel, and I've done a lot of shitty things in my life. I was nineteen when I killed for the first time, and quite frankly, I don't know if I'm even capable of loving somebody."

"They were all part of the game, right? No innocence bystanders or children I hope."

"Murder is murder, Megan, and no, I've never killed an ordinary civilian. However, even though the men I've killed were the scum of the earth, it still doesn't make it right."

"You see, the fact that you show remorse further lets me know you've changed, baby."

"I might have changed, but that still doesn't erase the crimes I've committed."

"All I know is what I feel, and I'm willing to go all the way with you. Give us a chance."

"I really like you, too, but let's take things slow...."

"Okay, I can live with that just as long as you remain in my life."

"I can't make you any promises regarding us, but I will give our friendship an honest chance to blossom."

"That's all that I ask. I'm willing to wait because I think you're worth it."

# Chapter 15

Today was the fateful day—the day that Stephanie and Brendan were supposed to exchange vows and pledge their undying love to each other. The only problem was the relationship was one-sided. Stephanie had confessed that she still loved me, and she also confessed to having an affair with Brendan's business partner, Marcus Doss. Brendan, on the other hand, was madly in love with Stephanie and clueless about what she was doing behind his back. I wanted no part of the wedding festivities of that day, and simply put, I just wanted to go home. Gabrielle promised to distance herself from Stephanie once the wedding was over, so I decided to take one for the team and suck it up.

I woke up horny as hell, and seeing Gabrielle half-naked in a t-shirt and thong panties didn't help the situation. I had a small window of opportunity to get a quickie in before the kids got up, so I decided to give her a breast massage to get her juices flowing. It utterly amazed me how sexy she still was after having four children, and we were definitely working on baby number five with the inordinate amount of sex we've been having lately.

I ignited a raging inferno after she started moaning a couple of minutes into the beginning of our *happy ending*. She then turned to face me, and we started kissing. This continued for several minutes before I inserted my index and middle finger into her flaming wetness and massaged her G-spot while sucking her erect nipples. Damn, she really turned me on.

I moved my way down to her love canal, removed her panties and worked my tongue and fingers until her climaxed. She then rolled me over on my back and said, "Let me blow out that candle, baby."

She gave me two and a half minutes of complete bliss before I lifted her t-shirt above her apple-shaped derriere and slid my joystick into her flaming walls. I made love to her slowly and steadily before picking up the pace. She matched me stroke for stroke—each pelvic thrust faster and more powerful than the previous one. We climaxed about fifteen minutes after our intense workout session began, and I collapsed next to her drenched in sweat.

"Damn, what a way to start out the day," I said.

"You always turn me on, baby," she said. "When you begin your day like this, it is very hard for anyone to get under your skin. If we could start out like this every day, I'd be the happiest woman in the world."

"I totally agree...if everybody could experience what we just experienced, I promise you there would be no more wars."

"You are so crazy, Maurice," she said jokingly. "I'mma get up and take my shower. Could you iron my white pants for me, baby?"

"Sure, no problem."

Gabrielle had mastered the art of charming a man, and it was one of the keys to our happy marriage. It was also the key to her getting almost anything she wanted from me. Sure, we had our disagreements like any other couple, but we never went to bed angry at each other. Our sex life was so good that I literally forgot about why we were arguing in the first place many times.

I started ironing her pants and took it a step further by ironing a matching blouse for her while she showered and glamorized herself up. I flexed my hand and realized that the pain was virtually gone—it was amazing what great sex could do.

She had to be at Stephanie's by eight and over to Brendan's to prep for the wedding. I had to get the kids dressed, and Gina was going to cook breakfast for them. Rick usually slept in, and today was no exception.

The wedding was scheduled to start at eleven, and I was going to ride with Malik and Erin in a limo over to Brendan's mansion in the far south suburbs. The itinerary of the day consisted of the wedding itself, the toast, dinner, live band and party. Brendan had asked me to be one of his groomsmen, but I graciously declined his offer. I lied and said that I couldn't commit to being in his wedding because August was my busiest month at the carwash and barbershop. He understood and didn't fret over it, but I wished I would've believed that he was on the up-and-up. My gut was leading me in the wrong direction because I should've been looking at Stephanie's ass instead of Brendan.

I had Gabrielle's pants and blouse neatly ironed and laid across the bed, and I went to check on the kids before Gabrielle got out the shower. It was a little after six-thirty, and Michael and Maurice Jr. weren't up yet. Alexa's eyes were opened, but she wasn't crying. I went to the kitchen to get one of her milk bottles, and I could hear Alexa whining once I got back upstairs.

"That's a good girl," I said as I picked her up and placed the bottle in her mouth.

I cradled her in my arms while she drank her milk, and went back to the room to see if Gabrielle was ready yet. She was already dressed when I got there.

"I see the little lady is already up," Gabrielle said.

"She's such a good baby," I said. "She wasn't even crying...she was just waiting patiently for her bottle."

"Give her to me, baby. When are Malik and Erin coming?"

"They'll be here at about nine. I'll have the boys dressed and fed by then."

"I'll get Alexa ready while you take your shower. Do you need anything ironed?"

"Yeah, babe, just a light iron on my shirt."

"Okay, I got you."

I grabbed my toothbrush, razor and towel and went to the bathroom. We ran our family like a well-oiled machine, and everything was second nature to us. Our everyday life consisted of a routine similar to this—we made sure Maurice Jr. and Michael were dressed and fed before I drove them to daycare. Jason was already self-sufficient, so my only job was dropping him off at school.

Gabrielle would take care of Alexa until it was time for her to go to her restaurant in downtown St. Louis at about noon. I would make my rounds to my carwash or barbershop after dropping off the boys, and I'd take any bank deposits from the previous days to the bank. I would alternate my visits to each spot every other day like clockwork.

I trusted my cousin Bobby to run the day-to-day operations of the carwash and my college roommate Will to run the entire barbershop while I kept the books for both businesses. I would fill in for either one of them whenever they needed time off, and now that I was retired from the game, I had a chance to rekindle my friendships with both of them. The three of us would hang out occasionally, and I've been renting out my condo to Will for the last three years after Gabrielle and I bought our first home.

We had a five-bedroom house in Clayton, MO; an upper-middle class neighborhood near Washington University. Neither one of us wanted or felt we needed a castle, so we agreed that Clayton was perfect place to raise our family.

Alexa would be mine for the rest of the day; and I'd pick up Jason, Michael and Maurice Jr. between three and four o'clock. I'd then cook their dinner and help Jason with his homework. Gabrielle would on occasion prepare dinner for us before she went to work. It was lights out for the kids by nine, and I had the rest of the evening to wind down and wait for Gabrielle to come home. She usually got home around eleven, and we'd talking about our day, make love and fall asleep in that order. This was my life, and as routine as it was, I loved every single minute of it. Gabrielle was about to leave when I finished grooming myself, and Gina was cooking breakfast and watching Alexa. I quickly got dressed so that I could see her off.

"I'll see you at the wedding," Gabrielle said.

"Alright, babe," I said, kissing her on the lips.

Gabrielle left, and I went in the kitchen to see what Gina was cooking. She had just finished the bacon, and the eggs were almost ready.

"Smells good," I said. "I'mma need a full stomach to deal with this shit."

"Yeah, I heard," Gina said. "Your girl Stephanie is foul."

"I don't disagree with you. I really don't want any part of this."

"Gabby is a better person than I am...if some chick told me that she was in love with Rick, I'd beat her ass for being too stupid to keep it to herself."

"You two are like night and day when it comes to shit like that...I don't think Gabby has ever had a fight in her life."

"Nah, she's always had me to fight her battles for her...she's a lover, not a fighter."

We all ate breakfast together once I got Michael and Maurice Jr. dressed and once Rick got up. Gina cooked enough for Malik and Erin to eat just in case they didn't eat breakfast yet. Gina was going to watch the kids while we were at the wedding, and Rick had a book signing downtown at noon. The boys and Alexa wore him out all week while Gina was at work, and the book signing was actually a break compared to watching our energetic kids.

Breakfast was great, and my morning treat with Gabrielle was beyond compare. I was off to a great start so far—but I knew that the storm was imminent.

# Chapter 16

Junior, Blaze and Peanut waited impatiently for the status of Bam's condition at the local hospital. Peanut was pacing back and worth, Blaze sat in the waiting room in deep thought, and Junior was off in a corner by himself. A doctor came to the waiting area to give them a status report on Bam's condition. The look in the doctor's eyes didn't put them at ease nor did it give them reason to be alarmed.

"I'm Dr. Brisket, can I speak to you all for a moment?" he asked.

"Sure doc, what's my man's condition?" Peanut asked before Blaze and Junior accompanied him.

"Your friend is stable, but he has a broken nose and a hairline fracture to his eye socket," the doctor answered. "He might need plastic surgery to repair the damage."

"So, he's gonna pull through, right?" Blaze asked.

"He's still in intensive care, and he has some swelling of the brain," the doctor answered. "He also has an enormous amount of alcohol in his system, and we won't anything for certain until the swelling goes down and alcohol dissipates."

"He might have brain damage?" Blaze asked.

"There's no way to be certain at this point," the doctor answered. "He took some kind of a beating...."

"Yes, he did," a man in a gray blazer and black slacks said before he flashed his badge. "I'm Detective Bryson, and this is my partner Detective Stevens. We're here to ask you guys some questions."

The doctor quietly excused himself while the three of them tried to win a staring contest with the detectives.

"Don't you all answer at once," Detective Bryson said.

"I don't have anything to say," Blaze said.

"I do," Peanut said, pointing at Junior. "This muthafucka here is responsible for the whole thing."

Detective Bryson looked in Junior's direction and said, "Is that true?"

"I'm not saying a damn thing without my lawyer present," Junior answered.

"People only lawyer up when they are guilty," Detective Stevens added.

"Oh, he's definitely guilty," Peanut said. "Y'all need to lock his ass up and throw away the fuckin' key."

"From the looks of things, I'm willing to bet all three of you degenerate motherfuckers have criminal records," Detective Bryson said, "and I have no problem making something stick to each one of you. So, you can make things easier on yourselves by answering our questions, or we can sort out this shit down at the station. I'll give you all a minute to decide."

Junior remained still while Peanut pulled Blaze to the side a few feet away. The detectives walked toward the nurse's station a few feet away in the opposite direction.

"We need to be on the same page, Blaze," Peanut whispered. "We have to collaborate our stories so that BJ's ass looks like a liar."

"What the fuck do you mean, Nut?" Blaze asked. "Bam got a beat down because he shot his brother...end of story, bruh."

"So what, cuz, you gonna take his side? Where's your fuckin' loyalty, man?"

"Right is right...friend or no friend, Bam is going to prison for the rest of his life if he pulls through."

"Fuck this Johnny-come-lately muthafucka...you need to remember who your real family is...."

"Alright, your minute is up," Detective Bryson said. "What's it going to be?"

"BJ right here beat my man half to death over a fuckin' bet," Peanut answered. "He's a sore loser who can't handle his goddamn liquor."

"Is that the truth," Detective Stevens asked, looking directly at Blaze.

Blaze looked back at Detective Stevens, then at Junior, and finally at Detective Bryson. He opened his mouth but couldn't find the words to speak.

"Come on, man, time's a wastin'," Detective Bryson said.

Blaze swallowed the lump in his throat and said, "Yeah, it's true."

"Well then, what do you have to say for yourself, BJ?" Detective Bryson asked.

"Not without my lawyer," Junior answered.

"Very well, have it your way," Detective Stevens said.

Detective Bryson read Junior his rights while Detective Stevens handcuffed him. Junior gave Blaze a cold stare that sent a chill through Blaze's entire body. Blaze had agonized over what he had just done and looked away in shame for lying to the police.

The detectives carted Junior off to the precinct for booking, and Peanut patted Blaze on the back for a job well done. All Blaze could do was stare in the direction of Junior and the detectives until they disappeared down the corridor and into one of the elevators. He lost yet another person close to him, and it rendered him numb and speechless. He walked back to the waiting area, sat down and buried his face into his hands. Peanut had joined him but remained silent.

Blaze was torn between staying loyal to his old friends by lying to keep Bam out of prison and doing the right thing by telling the truth about what really happened. He regretted every single detail of what had transpired that night and vowed to never get himself involved in a situation like that ever again.

# Chapter 17

Stephanie didn't have much to say on the ride to Brendan's and didn't remotely look like a bride-to-be. Gabrielle had waited for Stephanie to vent about what was on her mind and remained quiet for fear of rocking the boat and ruining her day. Jasmine was supposed to accompany them but got tied up. She planned on meeting Stephanie and Gabrielle at the house to help later.

Gabrielle couldn't take the silence anymore and said, "What's the matter, baby? You look like somebody died, girl."

"Somebody did," Stephanie answered. "I don't know if I can go through with this."

"You'll be fine...you probably just have jitters, that's all."

"What I have is definitely not wedding jitters. When I look in the mirror, I don't recognize the person staring back at me anymore. I have a great guy who I don't deserve."

"Where is all this coming from?"

"All come on, Gabrielle, like you don't already know. Maurice *had* to tell you what's going on with me."

"Yes, he did, Steph, but none of that matters because today is your day, and I'm gonna get you to the altar even if it kills me."

"But I don't love Brendan, and I can't fuck up his life. I have to come clean...."

"Come clean for whom, Brendan or yourself? Relieving your guilt will free you, but it will destroy him. He doesn't deserve that, so you have to find a way to forgive yourself and do right by him."

"How, Gabby? How do I do that? I can't turn my feelings on and off like that."

"Like getting over my husband?"

"Yes, like getting over your husband. Believe me, I wish to God I didn't feel this way, but I can't seem to do anything about it."

"Yes, you can, and you will. Brendan is a catch, and you need to start recognizing that fact. How would you feel if Jasmine or I made a play for him, or one of our other soros for that matter, huh?"

"I would definitely have a problem with that...."

"Well then...you see, you do have feelings for him, or else you would care if he saw other people. Look, you need to get it together and stop thinking about only yourself. Telling him the truth on your wedding day doesn't help anybody, and if you're truly done with Marc, focus on making Brendan happy from this point on."

"Thank you, I really needed to hear that. Thanks for talking some sense into me."

"I love you, girl, and I'd never try to steer you wrong."

"I love you, too. I'm okay...I think I can do this. Brendan loves me and we're going to have a great life together."

"Yes, you will. Just focus on your marriage and leave the foolishness behind."

Gabrielle had entered the expressway at 87$^{th}$ and the Dan Ryan—the westbound ride down 87$^{th}$ Street from South Chicago Avenue lasted about ten minutes.

"Where the hell is Jasmine?" Gabrielle asked. "I guess she expects me to do your makeup and chase the wedding planner around."

"She said she'll meet us there," Stephanie replied, "something about running a quick errand for her grandmother. She probably has to pick up her medication or something."

"Well, she better hurry up."

Gabrielle reached University Park in a little under a half hour and arrived at Brendan's place a few minutes later. They saw Jasmine's car in the driveway once they pulled up.

"What the fuck is she doing here?" Stephanie asked. "It's no way she got here this fast."

"She lied," Gabrielle answered. "Something is going on, and we're gonna get to the bottom of it."

They jumped out of the car and stormed up to Brendan's front door. Stephanie rang the door incessantly before the butler answered it.

"Where the hell is Brendan?" Stephanie asked.

"Calm down, ma'am," the butler answered. "He's in his study. Follow me."

The butler led them down the hallway surrounded by antique paintings, luxurious furnishings and marble flooring. When they reached his study, he was on the phone.

"What the fuck is going on, Brendan?" Stephanie abruptly asked. "Where's Jasmine?"

"I'll call you right back," Brendan said. "What's wrong, baby?"

"Don't baby me, goddammit," Stephanie answered. "I turn my back for five seconds and you fuck my best friend!"

"What are you talking about, Stephanie?" Brendan asked feeling perplexed. "Jasmine's here to see my brother Ricardo...they have been seeing each other since the wedding rehearsal."

"Then why is it a secret?" Stephanie asked. "She better not be in your bedroom...."

"You need to get a grip, Steph," Gabrielle said. "He said she's with Ricardo. Let it go."

"Well, I going to find them," Stephanie said before she stormed off.

"What hell is wrong with her, Gabrielle?" Brendan asked.

"I think she has jitters, that's all," Gabrielle answered.

# Chapter 18

We had just finished eating breakfast about ten minutes before Malik and Erin arrived, and they didn't waste anytime fixing themselves a plate. Gina took the kids shopping to get them some toys and some clothes, and she wanted to be done before the early afternoon. I was putting on my tux when the doorbell rang. Malik and Erin were already eating by the time I got back downstairs. Rick had let them in before heading over to his book signing.

"Hey, you two," I said. "You all didn't waste anytime, huh?"

"I was starving, and the food smelled good," Malik said.

"Gina sure can burn," Erin added. "Where is she?"

"She took the kids shopping," I answered. "She wants to get there as soon as the mall opens."

"Good idea," Erin said. "I don't like crowds much, either."

"I can't tell," Malik blurted out. "Seems like you're in the stores every other day."

"For your information, I shop at exclusive stores, you know, *price upon request* establishments," Erin said, testy from Malik's comment. "If you have to ask, you can't afford it."

"Hell, you really can't afford it," Malik said.

"You don't know what I can afford," Erin countered. "You-are-not my daddy."

"Come on you two," I said, "this isn't the way to start the day."

"You're right, my friend, and I'm done with it," Malik said. "So, is there trouble in paradise with Stephanie?"

"Yeah, how you know?" I asked.

"I overheard blabbermouth over there," Malik answered.

"You need to get some business," Erin said. "I don't ease drop when you're talking to one of your hoes, do I?"

"You really need to stop doing that," Malik said. "For the *very* last time, I'm not cheating on you."

"Please don't ruin my day, y'all," I said. "Erin, what did Gabby tell you?"

"She told me Stephanie's sneaking around," Erin answered. "I'm so glad you chose Gabby over her, Maurice."

"Yeah, she's creeping, but she should've broke it off with Marc last night," I said.

"She needs to come clean and tell Brendan the truth," Erin said. "I'd wanna know if somebody was creeping on me."

"I doubt if she's gonna do that," I said. "Something tells me that she's gonna marry him and act like nothing ever happened."

"Are you gonna tell Brendan?" Malik asked me.

"It's not my place," I said. "He's really not my friend."

"So, somebody has to be your friend for you to do the right thing?" Erin asked.

"What is the *right* thing, Erin?" I asked. "Who made you the judge and jury? Just stay out of it, okay?"

"I'm just here for a wedding and a good time," Erin said. "You won't hear a word out of me."

"Good," I said. "You all ready to go?"

"Yeah, let's head on over there," Malik answered.

# Chapter 19

Mike had an early day that began with a trip to his barbershop to open up before heading over to the recording studio to check on Junior's progress with the album. He had Junior's single debuting on the radio that day, and he felt it was finally his turn to shine. He owed his dream of owning his record label to his drug connect, Donnie Lucas. Donnie gave him the money after a botched drug deal in LA three years ago as a favor to his long time associate, Darius Clinton, who was also his cousin. He then took a half million dollars and formed Rhymes and Lyrics Records.

He was the type of person who loved to flaunt his wealth and act larger than what he really was. Truth be told, he was small-time and would always be small-time. He ran a successful barbershop, moved a few kilos here and there, and his record label net him a moderate return. He was a worker bee—a small fish in a big pond. He did have some leadership qualities, but his biggest asset was the gift of gab. He was known all across each borough in New York City, but his popularity wasn't necessarily because of anything he did—he got respect based on his cousin Darius's reputation, not his own.

He would faithfully receive a call every month telling him the time and place of the shipment of drugs coming in on the boat for Lucas. He would then handle transporting the shipment from the dock to the warehouse, and he would never have direct contact with Lucas.

His burner rang, and he answered if after parking his car on the side of the street.

"We're havin' a party tonight and you're invited," the voice said.

"Oh, yeah?" Mike asked. "Same time and place?"

"Yeah, make sure you bring your own bottle."

He disconnected the call and arrived at his barbershop that was a half of a mile from Flatbush Avenue on Linden Boulevard in Brooklyn a few minutes later. He had taken all of the risk in bringing the shipment to Lucas's warehouse each month, and in turn, Lucas would sell him a few kilos at the wholesale price for his services.

Two of his barbers were standing by the entrance waiting for him to open.

"What's up, Mike?" Omar said, giving him some dap.

"I can't call it," Mike answered. "What's good with you, Ali?"

"It's all good, son," Ali answered. "What time are you going to the studio today?"

"In about an hour," Mike answered. "Why?"

"I want you to listen to my demo," Ali answered.

"I told you that you need to practice your flow before I sign you, Ali," Mike said. "You sound like one of them wack-ass country bamas, no offense."

"Just listen to it, Mike," Ali pleaded. "I promise you it won't be a waste of time."

"Alright, I'll listen to it, but if you shit ain't up to par, I ain't giving you another chance," Mike said.

"Fair enough," Ali said.

"Damn your music, Ali," Omar said, "what about that package, Mike?"

"It'll be here tonight at the dock around six," Mike answered. "I got the call a few minutes ago."

"Good, because I'm almost dry," Omar said. "How many bricks you gonna get?"

"I got money for ten," Mike answered.

"Cool, that's what's up," Omar said.

"Where are those other two boneheads?" Mike asked.

"Joe said he's running late, and Terrell won't be here today," Omar said.

"Damn, that's the third time this week," Mike said. "If Terrell keeps this shit up, I'mma give his spot to someone else."

"It's that new chick he's fuckin' with," Ali said. "She's wearing his whupped ass out."

"Well, he better get his shit together," Mike said. "We lose business when people have to wait because we're backed up."

The three of them spent about ten minutes waiting before the first customer walked in. The guy was Omar's client, so Mike decided to give Junior a call. It went straight to voicemail, but he didn't leave a message. He called Blaze afterward, and he picked up on the third ring.

"What's up, Blaze?" Mike asked. "You at the studio?"

"Nah, boss man," Blaze answered. "We got trouble."

"What kind of trouble?"

"It's BJ, he got locked up."

"Locked up?! How the fuck that happen?!"

"Not over the phone...I'll be by the shop in a few minutes."

"Hurry your ass up, man."

Mike ended the call and pounded his fist into the wall.

"Fuck!" Mike shouted.

"Yo, Mike, what's wrong?" Ali asked.

"My number one moneymaker is locked up," Mike answered.

"How did he get knocked, son?" Omar asked.

"I don't fuckin' know, but Blaze's dumb ass better tell me something," Mike answered.

Omar continued to cut his client's hair while Mike waited for Blaze to get there, and Ali kept busy by sweeping the floor. Blaze walked in with Peanut ten minutes later.

"What the fuck happened, man?" Mike asked.

"We were up all night playing Madden, and BJ got into a fight with my boy, Bam," Blaze answered. "He fucked him up really bad, and *one-time* arrested him at the hospital."

"*One-time*?" Mike asked. "Who called the cops?"

"I don't know," Blaze replied, "probably somebody on the hospital staff."

"This shit doesn't sound right, Blaze," Mike said. "Why would BJ beat the shit outta your boy over a stupid football game? He has too much riding on his album to bug out like that."

"Everybody had a little too much to drink," Peanut replied. "BJ lost the bet and snapped off."

"You vouch for your man?" Mike asked.

"Yeah, that's how it went down," Blaze answered. "He don't like to lose, and he went ballistic when my man took his money."

"Come on, let's go bail him out," Mike said.

"Nah, I can't go," Blaze lied. "I gotta take Sally to the doctor at noon."

"Well, where the fuck he at?!" Mike asked angrily.

"At the station a few blocks from the hospital," Blaze replied.

Blaze and Peanut left, and Mike hurried to his office to grab some cash.

"Alright, I'm out, fellas," Mike said. "Here, Omar, lock up for me when y'all are done. I don't know when or if I'mma be back today."

"Don't worry about it, boss," Ali said. "We got your back."

"Yeah, Mike," Omar said. "We got you. BJ's a cool dude, so I hope everything is okay."

"Thanks," Mike said. "I'll give y'all an update as soon as I know something. *One*."

"*One love*, boss man," Omar and Ali said in unison.

He rushed out to his car and sped off. He had hoped he had enough cash to cover bail, and he was determined to not let anything mess up his cash cow, Junior.

# Chapter 20

Junior sat in a six by eight cell awaiting arraignment after being fingerprinted and photographed. He never imagined being locked up yet again and was pissed at himself for losing control. There were three other guys waiting patiently in the holding cell—neither one of them in much of a mood for conversation like him. He felted betrayed by Blaze because they had developed a good working relationship and friendship, but he soon learned that Blaze's true loyalty was to his homeboys.

One of the guys kept staring at Junior but would look away whenever he returned the stare. Finally, the guy mustered up enough courage to say something.

"Yo, aren't you *Ice Cold*?" the guy asked.

"Yeah, I am," Junior answered.

"Man, I heard that cut with Delilah on it...the shit is off the chain, son."

"Thanks, man."

"Raheem...my name is Raheem."

"Nice to meet you, Raheem."

"When does the album drop?"

"My single drops today...it should be on Hot 97 this afternoon."

"That's what's up."

Raheem paused, looked at Junior's right hand and asked, "Yo, somebody took a serious ass whuppin', huh?"

"Look, Raheem, I rather not talk about it," Junior answered. "I appreciate the friendly conversion, but I'm really not in the mood for anymore talking."

"No disrespect...I understand."

The four of them resumed sitting in silence for several minutes more before a correctional officer walked up to their cell and said, "You have a visitor, Ousley."

Junior left with the CO, and he led him to the visiting area. There was a family to the left talking to one of the inmates, and an inmate and his girlfriend were laughing and talking to the immediate right of the family. Mike was sitting at another one of the tables to the right of the family waiting for him.

"What's up, BJ?" Mike asked.

"You tell me," Junior answered. "What did Blaze say to you?"

"He said you lost your cool, my dude. Come on, BJ, you're my number one man...if I lose you, the label dies."

"Not my finest hour, I admit, but I'm sure he didn't tell you the whole story."

"I came to bail you out and hear your side of it."

"I can't talk before my sister gets here from DC, Mike, but I will say that you need to drop Blaze's sorry ass."

"Why should I drop him? You were the one that snapped off over a fuckin' bet."

"Is that what he told you? Come on, you know me better than that."

"Yeah, I admit it doesn't make sense, son, so what the fuck happened?"

"I'll tell you everything once my bail is set, and I get out of here."

"That's fair. So, your sister is a big-time attorney, right?"

"Yeah, she's a bulldog in the courtroom, but if Blaze's boy dies, it won't make a difference."

"Say word...well, I'll be back to post your bail in a couple of hours. I got some other business to take care of right now...."

"You don't have to worry about that...Nikki will bond me out once she gets here."

"Don't be ridiculous, BJ, you're my number one artist, and I always take care of my artists."

"Whatever, man, one."

"One love, homie."

# Chapter 21

Gabrielle had managed to calm Stephanie down from her earlier tirade before the three of us got there. Stephanie's cheating had distorted her thinking, and she couldn't wrap her brain around Brendan being totally faithful to her because of her own guilt.

The three of us were red-carpet ready even though neither of us was in the wedding. Malik and I had on black tuxedos with a black tie and cummerbund, and Erin had on a black evening gown, a diamond necklace and bracelet that accentuated her ten-karat wedding ring, and six-inch black stilettos. Our intent wasn't to upstage the bride and groom, but we all looked damn good.

We arrived at Brendan's just before ten thirty, and the people were starting to roll in. Brendan and Stephanie stressed an eleven o'clock sharp start, but no wedding I ever attended began on time. We took our seats in Brendan's spacious backyard that had about one hundred fifty chairs symmetrically placed forming an aisle leading up to the makeshift altar. Stephanie had invited about seventy people, and Brendan's list was about the same—anyone who arrived too late was going to have to stand because seats were filling up fast. The noise elevated several octaves, and Gabrielle emerged from the crowd and walked toward us.

"Hey, baby," Gabrielle said as I stood from my seat and gave her a kiss. "How's everybody doing?"

"I'm great," Erin answered, hugging her.

"Hey, Gabby," Malik said, kissing her on the cheek. "How's the bride?"

"A nervous wreck," Gabrielle answered, "but she'll be alright. When did you all get here?"

"A few minutes ago," I said. "So, she's really gonna go through with it, huh?"

"Yeah, is she gonna come clean and tell this poor guy the truth?" Erin asked.

"Huh?" Gabrielle huffed. "I can't believe you two. This isn't the time or the place for that."

"I'm not saying a thing," I said.

"You don't have anything to say, Malik?" Gabrielle asked.

"Nope," Malik replied, "not my place to say anything."

"You all need to take notes from Malik," Gabrielle said.

"No, what you need to do is talk some sense into your girl," Erin said. "Stephanie's out the box, Gabby."

"It's my job to support Stephanie, not judge her," Gabrielle said. "I'm in no position to give anybody advice."

"Right is right, Gabby, and Stephanie needs to come clean," Erin said. "It's not proper to be in Brendan's face and pretend like nothing has happened. I'm not built that way."

"Me, either," I said, "but we need to stay out of it. The truth will come out eventually."

"I agree," Malik added. "If Stephanie can live with it, so can I."

"Typical of you," Erin said. "Your happy-go-lucky ass never takes a stand on anything."

"You never had a problem with it before," Malik said.

"Enough, you two," I interjected. "Let's just let everything play out...none of us are perfect."

"Right, baby," Gabrielle said. "Everybody just sit tight and let nature take its course. I have to get back...I'll talk to you all later."

Gabrielle went back inside to tend to Stephanie's needs before the wedding. We then waited for the wedding to start. Of course, it didn't start on time because the best man misplaced the rings. Go figure.

I had zoned out for a brief instance—reminiscing about my own wedding day—the day Gabrielle and I exchanged vows in my hospital bed three weeks after I got shot. My heart was homesick to a place I'd never been until I met her on that fateful day in college, and I was never the same after that.

Our wedding reflected who we were—it was simple—and only ten close friends and family stood by my bed while Gabrielle and I began the next chapter of our lives. Our immediate families were there—Rick and Gina from Gabrielle's family; and Erin, Malik, Junior, Nicole and Dad from my family. Stephanie and Agent Stanton were there, and Gabrielle and Stephanie's mutual friend and sorority sister Jasmine was also present. We made my hospital room a small spectacle that I'd remember for the rest of my life.

A tap on my shoulder quickly snapped me out of my daydream, and Stephanie's father Mr. Davison was standing in front of us. He was a distinguished-looking man who exemplified high society—a tall, light-skinned, and clean-shaven man with salt-and-pepper hair. He also sported wire rim glasses, a charcoal-gray Brooks Brothers suit and Giovanni Marquez loafers. I stood up to greet him.

"Hello, sir," I said, shaking his hand firmly.

"Hello, Maurice," Mr. Davison said. "Great to see you again."

"Likewise," I said. "This is my sister Erin and my brother-in-law Malik, and this is Stephanie's father."

"Nice to meet you both," Mr. Davison said, shaking Erin's hand and then Malik's hand. "I'm a huge fan, Malik."

"Thank you, sir," Malik said.

"Can I talk to you for a minute inside, Maurice?" Mr. Davison asked.

"Sure, Mr. Davison," I replied. "Don't let anybody take my seat, you two."

"I got you," Malik said.

I grudgingly walked with Mr. Davison toward the back door, and I could still hear Malik and Erin arguing on the way inside.

"*I'm a huge fan, Malik,*" Erin mocked Mr. Davison. "Does he know who I am? I'm only an Oscar-nominee and platinum recording artist."

"Maybe he doesn't watch a lot television or listen to R&B," Malik said.

"Don't patronize me, Malik," Erin said. "He knew who you were."

"Okay, so he's a basketball fan, damn," Malik cried. "Everything isn't always about you...people don't always recognize me either, but I don't make a big deal about it."

"Whatever," Erin said sarcastically.

I shut the door behind us and asked, "What do you want to talk about, Mr. Davison?"

"I just want to apologize for the way I treated you in the past," he answered. "My family and I never gave you a chance, and totally ashamed of myself for that."

"You're right," I said, "you and your family never gave me a chance, and Stephanie and I weren't strong enough to overcome the adversity. However, sir, I don't believe in holding grudges, and I accept your apology."

"Thank you, Maurice. Brendan seems like a nice guy and all, but I regret that you're not my son-in-law instead."

"I appreciate you saying that, but it wasn't meant to be. I'm happily married to a beautiful woman, and I have four wonderful children."

"Yes, I know, to Gabrielle. She's a lovely young woman."

There was momentary silence, and Mr. Davison said, "So, you're been through quite a bit these last few years, most notably your shooting and now the attempted plane hijacking. How are you holding it together?"

"Day by day, sir," I answered. "Life has a whole new meaning to me these days...I live a simple, quiet life; and I love it."

"That's good to hear."

"I extended my hand to him and said, "Well, it was nice talking to you, sir. Take care."

"Take care, Maurice," he said, shaking my hand once again.

I stepped back outside and reclaimed my seat. I managed to keep it short and to the point with Mr. Davison, and no daggers were thrown. Job well done. Malik and Erin both looked disgusted with each other and weren't talking. My sister hated not being the center of attention, and it was beginning to drive Malik nuts.

The backyard was now filled to capacity, and it was almost eleven. I noticed Jasmine briefly peeking out the back door to see who was in attendance, and then she walked back to the room where the bridesmaids were getting ready.

"Girl, everybody and their mama is out there," Jasmine said. "We really need to hurry it up."

"I'm almost done with Steph's makeup," Gabrielle said.

"You okay?" Stephanie's sister Marie asked.

"No, but I will be," Stephanie answered.

"What do you mean, *no*?" Marie asked. "This is supposed to be the happiest day of your life, Stephanie."

"Don't start, Marie," Stephanie replied. "I'm nervous enough as it is...and what do you know about it anyway? You and your ex never even made it to the altar."

"Wow, Stephanie, how could you say something like that to me at a time like this?" Marie said, stung by Stephanie's remark.

"Behave, you two," Gabrielle interjected. "Everything's gonna be fine."

"Where's Ciera and Brittany?" Jasmine asked. "We should be walking down the aisle this very minute."

"They went to check on the guys," Gabrielle answered. "We're only a few minutes behind schedule."

The other two bridesmaids Ciera and Brittany finally came back to the room, and Ciera said, "Clarence is here with the rings. We can get started."

"There, take a look at yourself in the mirror, Steph," Gabrielle said. "You look beautiful."

"Yes, you *do* look so beautiful," Jasmine added.

"Come on, little sis," Marie said, "See how beautiful Gabrielle made you look in the mirror."

Stephanie stood up and examined herself in the mirror for a moment before turning to Gabrielle.

"Thank you, Gabby," Stephanie said. "Thank you for everything. I love how I look."

"No problem, girl. I got you," Gabrielle said.

"Come on, let's get started," Brittany said.

The ceremony began about ten minutes later, and the flower girls walked down the aisle first. One of the flower girls was Marie's daughter, Tiara. The bridesmaids and groomsmen were next, and finally, Stephanie and Mr. Davison. Brendan and Clarence turned to face Stephanie and her father as they made their way up to the altar. Mr. Davison placed Stephanie's hand in Brendan's hand and sat next to Stephanie's mom in the front row. Stephanie handed Jasmine her bouquet of flowers as Jasmine lifted back her veil.

You couldn't have asked for a better day—not too hot and not too cool. The sun was out without a cloud in the sky, and a gentle breeze blew every so often.

The minister started off by saying a few introductory words before getting into it.

"If anyone present knows of any reason why this couple shouldn't be married, speak now or forever hold your peace," the minister said.

Marc then made eye contact with Stephanie once she turned her head in his direction, and he smiled suggestively before winking at her. Brendan turned around at the same time Stephanie looked in the direction of the groomsmen and saw what Marc had done. Brendan angrily stepped toward Marc, but Ricardo and Clarence blocked his path so that he couldn't get to him.

"What the hell was that, Marc?" Brendan asked.

"What are you talking about, Brendan?" Marc asked.

"You know what I'm talking about," Brendan answered. "I know what I saw, and you got some explaining to do."

"Calm down, bro," Clarence urged. "It must be some misunderstanding or something."

"Nah, Clarence, this bastard winked at Stephanie, and I want to know why," Brendan said.

"Huh?" Ricardo asked nobody in particular. "What the hell is wrong with you, Marc?"

"How dare you make a mockery out of my daughter's wedding, young man," Mr. Davison stood up and said, directing his comment at Marc. "How dare you make a pass at my daughter."

"You were my friend and business partner, Marc," Brendan stated, "and you turn around and do this. Stephanie, what's going on, baby?"

Stephanie's eyes became watery, and she quivered when she spoke, "I'm sorry, baby...I'm so sorry...."

"Sorry for what, Stephanie?" Brendan asked with a painful expression on his face.

"Marc and I were having an affair," Stephanie said remorsefully. "I hope you can forgive me."

Most everyone in the yard sighed *oh* simultaneously, and everyone was stunned. Brendan stood motionless momentarily before turning toward Marc and punching him in the jaw. Marc fell to the ground, and Brendan stood over him and shouted, "You are a low-down, backstabbing bastard, Marc!"

Brendan turned to face Stephanie with fire in his eyes and said, "I never want to see you again!"

Brendan then stormed out the yard, got into his car and sped away. Stephanie then ran inside of the house and locked herself in one of the rooms.

"Damn," I said. "I can't believe what just happened."

"That's goes double for me," Malik added. "That dude is foul, man. Who does that?"

"With friends like that, who needs enemies?" Erin asked the two of us. "Baby, I'm sorry I've been acting like such a brat...I love you so much."

"I love you, too," Malik said. "I promise you that you will never have to worry about something like this happening to us."

"I glad to hear you two still love each other, but we need to tend to Stephanie," I said.

The three of us walked toward Gabrielle and the other bridesmaids who were still in a state of shock from what had just taken place, and we watched the rest of the drama unfold. Marc tried to pick himself up off of the ground only to be decked again by Ricardo. Clarence prevented Ricardo from doing any further damage by restraining him.

"That's for my brother, you son of a bitch," Ricardo said.

"That's enough!" the minister said. "This is no way to behave at a wedding ceremony."

"Yeah, he's not worth it, man," Clarence said. "He'll get his one day."

With mouth now bleeding and left eye swollen, Marc then tried to remove himself from the scene again only to be stopped in his tracks by Mr. Davison.

"Not so fast, young man," Mr. Davison said.

"What, you want to hit me, too?" Marc asked.

"No, I'm not going to hit you," Mr. Davison replied. "As much as I want to hit you, it's not going to help the situation. However, I am going to make your life a living hell, though."

"Oh yeah, how do you plan on doing that?" Marc asked. "The last time I checked, I was a millionaire who ran my own company."

"Wrong," Mr. Davison replied. "I'll personally see to it that you never work in the financial industry in Chicago or anywhere else ever again once Brendan is done with you. You're finished, son."

Marc gave Mr. Davison an angry look before walking away without saying another word. I gave Gabrielle a hug after all of the commotion and said, "You need to go see about your girl before she does something crazy."

"I know," Gabrielle said. "I can't believe what just happened here."

"Believe it, baby," I said. "No matter how hard you try, you can't run away from the truth."

# Chapter 22

Darius was sound asleep on the passenger's side while Megan entered New York city limits. He had finally relinquished control of the steering wheel once his vision became blurry from fatigue hours ago. Megan was lost as she found herself on the Henry Hudson Bridge. She tapped Darius on the shoulder to wake him.

"I think you need to take over," Megan said. "I don't have any idea where I'm going."

"It's okay, babe," Darius said reassuringly. "You can get off at the next exit so that we can get some gas, and we can get a room somewhere nearby."

"What's the next move?" Megan asked. "Freshen up? Have sex?"

"Yeah, all in that order," Darius replied, laughing and shaking his head, "but remember why we're here in the first place. I only plan on us staying for a few hours, and once I find Donnie, we're out."

"I hear you," Megan said in a seductive tone, "but all business and no pleasure makes you a dull boy."

"Duly noted, beautiful. Pull over at this gas station, and we can get something to eat before we get a room if you're hungry."

"The only thing I'm hungry for is you...we need to finish what we started, big boy."

Megan pulled up in a Shell gas station, and Darius went inside the store to buy the gas and some food and beverages. There was a Motel 6 a half block down the road, so everything they needed was right in the general vicinity. Darius pumped the gas, and then they left for the motel.

"I got us some sandwiches and pop," Darius said.

"That's good, baby," Megan said. "Seriously, though, what's the plan? When are we gonna look for Donnie?"

"We can start searching for him tonight," Darius answered. "It's this spot in Harlem where he hangs out, so we can start there."

"What's the name of the club?"

"It's called Billie's Black Bar Lounge. We can swing by there at around six."

They checked in under Megan's name and went to their room. As soon as Darius placed their bags on the floor, Megan tackled him onto the bed and kissed him fiercely. He met her passion with equal force before she worked her way down to his groan. She then ripped his pants and boxers off, and she began treating herself to an early dessert.

"Wait, baby," Darius said before he took off his shirt and completely stripped her down.

He lay on his back and pulled her shapely bottom toward his face and indulged in her cookies while she indulged in his.

"Oh, baby, that feels soooo good," Megan cried out. "I wanna feel you inside of me, daddy."

She straddled him with her back to his face and began rocking her hips back and forth. He placed both his hands on her hips and pulled her toward him with each stroke making the penetration deeper.

"Oooh, you're so big," Megan moaned. "Fuck me harder, baby."

She rode him for about five minutes before grabbing his hands and pulling him upright so that he could stroke her from behind. Their pelvic thrusts then became more rapid and more powerful, and Darius spouted off like a water faucet before falling back on the bed. Megan slid over next to him, and he kissed her on her forehead and wrapped his arms around her. She placed her right hand in his—fingers intertwined.

"That was a little better, wasn't it?" he asked, looking for some sort of reassurance or approval.

"You were absolutely incredible, baby," she answered, trying to stroke his ego. "You're all the man I could ever want."

"Aw, you're just saying that...just tell me the truth. I know I'm not the lover I used to be."

"No, baby, I mean it...you were awesome. Trust me, if it was bad, I'd definitely tell you."

"Well, then, thank you, sweetheart."

"You're very welcome."

They continued to cuddle next to each other and forgot about the sandwiches on the dresser. Before they knew it, they were fast asleep.

# Chapter 23

The same CO had come to get Junior a second time once Nicole arrived from Washington, DC; but the guard lead him to a private room where she was waited for him instead. She got up and gave Junior a firm hug, and the guard left.

"What have you gotten yourself into, boy?" Nicole inquired in her mother-like tone. "You owe me big time."

"I know, sis," Junior said apologetically. "I still can't believe I'm even in this mess."

"What the hell happened? I want every single detail of that night."

Junior gave her the entire spill from the time he first left the studio with Delilah to the altercation at Blaze's apartment, and finally, the hospital. She shook her head in disapproval once he finished and asked, "Did you say anything to the police?"

"I'm well versed in standard police procedure, so the answer is no," Junior answered.

"Don't get smart, BJ. Do you realize what you're up against?"

"Yes, sis, I do. If that guy dies, I could spend the rest of my life in prison. I'm sure I'm being charged with aggravated assault and battery and attempted murder, right?"

"Yes, you are, so we have to think of a game plan. Now, you said that this guy admitted to shooting Maurice in LA, but the other two witnesses at the hospital denied it, correct?"

"Technically yes, because I didn't refute what they said I did to the cops."

"Okay, here's what we're going to do. You are going to plead not guilty by way of self-defense because after you said *'I'll kill you'* in a fit of rage, the guy Bam charged you and swung on you before you knocked him to the ground, and the other guy Peanut came at you before you knocked him out cold."

"But I struck Bam repeated while he was lying unconscious on the floor because I really did want to kill his ass."

Nicole gave him a stern look and said, "We can say that you feared for your life because both men were reputed gang members, and you wanted to make sure he was out cold before Blaze pulled you off of him."

"Alright sis, we'll go with that even though it's not entirely the truth."

"In the immortal words of Denzel Washington, '*do you want to go to jail, or do you want to go home*,' stupid?"

"Alright, Nikki, alright. That's why you make the big bucks, Ms. high-priced attorney."

"That's right, and don't you forget it. You know, you really need to watch the company you keep because you have too much to lose."

"You absolutely right...it was poor judgement on my part."

"What's done is done...come on...I pulled some strings to get your case bumped up. Your arraignment starts in five minutes."

The CO led them to the courtroom, and they waited for their case to be called. Five minutes later, the court officer called their docket number.

"The People of the State of New York against Brent Ousley Jr.," the court officer said.

The bailiff brought Junior in front of the judge where the defendants stand, and Nicole stood next to him. The prosecuting attorney stood on the right side of them while the judge reviewed Junior's file. The judge then motioned for the prosecutor to give him the customary notices of the arraignment.

"One-Ninety-Fifty, Your Honor," the prosecutor said.

"Cross-One-Ninety-Fifty, Your Honor," Nicole said moments later after the judge made eye contact with her.

The prosecutor stated in code that it was a felony case, and Nicole countered by stating in code that she was reserving Junior's right to testify before a Grand Jury. The judge then asked the prosecutor if he thought bail should be set.

"This young man has proven that he's a menace to society with a previous conviction for drug and weapons charges in the state of Illinois," the prosecutor said. "Moreover, he just beat a man half to death. Mr. Ousley shouldn't be allowed to freely walk the streets of New York, therefore I recommend that bail be denied."

"Do you have anything to add, counselor?" the judge asked Nicole.

"Yes, Your Honor, may I state that my client is not a menace to society," Nicole stated. "Mr. Ousley is a rising star in the music industry who has everything to lose and would not jeopardize his future without just cause. He has paid his debt to society and was merely acting in self-defense when two reputed gang members attacked him on the night in question. I recommend that Mr. Ousley be released on recognizance."

"Bail will be set at $100,000," judge ordered.

The prosecutor was visibly upset after the judge's decision while Nicole and Junior remained calm and kept their composure. Nicole then paid the clerk, and the two of them left the police station.

"You're not out of the woods yet," Nicole warned. "It's going to be your word against theirs...I have to somehow get one of them to admit that Bam shot your brother in front of a jury and get the judge to bring them all up on perjury charges."

"This is true, Nikki," Junior affirmed, "and all I can do at this point is pray about it. I also wanna say thank you for coming to my rescue."

"You're welcome, BJ," Nicole said. "I could never turn my back on you."

Nicole dropped Junior off at the studio about twenty minutes later. He needed to retrieve his car from the previous night.

"Wanna get something to eat?" Junior asked. "I'm starving."

"Nah, I have to get to the airport," Nicole answered. "I'm in the middle of a very important murder case, and I still have a ton of work to do."

"I understand. I really appreciate what you do, sis. You're the hardest working person I know."

"Thank you, BJ. I'll see you in a few weeks so that we can come up with a game plan to get you out of this mess."

"Okay, sis, see you next month."

Junior kissed Nicole on the cheek and got out of her car. He waved at her as she drove off, and he got in his car and sat for a brief moment. He then decided to give Delilah a call. Her phone went to voicemail after several rings.

"Hey, babe, give me a call when you're free," he said. "You won't believe the night I've had."

# Chapter 24

Gabrielle, Jasmine, Marie and Stephanie's mother Mrs. Davison had taken turns trying to get through to Stephanie, but she wouldn't bulge. Malik, Erin, Mr. Davison and I stood by a few feet away from them. She locked herself in their bedroom—the bedroom that they were going to spend the rest of their lives sleeping in. Thirty minutes had passed, and we could still hear Stephanie's sobs through the door.

"Stephanie please," Mrs. Davison pleaded, "please come out and talk to us, baby."

"Go away!" Stephanie cried. "Just leave me alone!"

I, on the other hand, felt more sympathetic toward Brendan than I felt toward Stephanie. She was the one who had trashed the relationship, and now she was feeling overwhelming regret. A part of me wanted to reach out and comfort Stephanie, but the other half of me felt that she made her own bed.

"Do something, Maurice," Gabrielle urged. "You have to get through to her."

"Do what, Gabby?" I asked. "I don't know what to say, and besides, I don't feel it's my place."

Mr. Davison put his hand on my shoulder and said, "Stephanie needs you, Maurice. Nobody knows her better than you do."

With a persuasive push from Mr. Davison, I knocked on the door and said, "Stephanie, it's me. Open up."

"I said go away, Maurice!" Stephanie shouted. "I can't face you or anybody else right now."

"Look, Stephanie, you're going to have to come out here someday," I said. "I just want to talk to you, that's all. Nobody is judging you...."

"Just leave me alone, please," Stephanie said.

"Come on, Steph, you're better than this," I said. "The Stephanie that I know would never back down to any challenge. Things are not as bad as they seem to be."

There was then silence, and moments later, Brendan's father walked up to Mr. Davison and said, "Your daughter ruined everything, and what she did was totally inexcusable."

"You're absolute right, and I'm terrible sorry, Mr. Moss," Mr. Davison said. "On behalf of my family, please accept my apology."

"I'm afraid I can't do that," Mr. Moss said. "You and your daughter will never be a part of my family, and you all need to leave my son's house now."

Mr. Moss stormed away, and all of us stood by still in shock from what had just happened. Stephanie still hadn't come out of the room, and I walked over to Mr. Davison and said, "I'm sorry, Mr. Davison, but Stephanie won't talk to me."

"It's okay, son," Mr. Davison said. "Thanks for trying."

Stephanie finally unlocked the door several minutes later and came out of the room to face us. Her mascara was ruined—her excessive crying left black streaks down her face from her eyes to her chin. She walked directly toward Mr. Davison to receive his embrace. She was truly a daddy's girl.

"I'm so sorry, Daddy," she sobbed. "I disgraced the entire family, and I hope you can forgive me."

"Everything's going to be okay, baby girl," Mr. Davison said, kissing her on her forehead. "Come on, let's go home."

Mr. and Mrs. Davison left with Stephanie and her sister Marie, and the rest of us walked toward the front of Brendan's house. Our limo wasn't due back until much later, so Erin started to make the call to have the driver return for them. However, Gabrielle stopped her because she had Gina's Range Rover.

"Why are you calling the limo service?" Gabrielle asked. "We can take you all back to your Dad's house."

"I didn't want to impose," Erin answered.

"Don't be silly," Gabrielle insisted. "You're family, so it's no trouble at all. Besides, we need to see Dad before we go back to St. Louis."

"Maybe you should call the limo back, Erin," I said. "I need to try to find Brendan and smooth things over. I don't like the way things ended, and I need to apologize to him. Can you ride with them, Gabby?"

"Sure, baby, no problem," Gabrielle replied.

"Okay," I said. "I'll come out to Dad's when I'm done. See you all later."

"Wait," Malik said. "Do you need some backup?"

"Nah, bro, I'm good," I replied.

I left Brendan's and headed to a place not far away from there. He was probably drowning his sorrows at Dave's Spot, a sports bar we frequented from time to time. I had no idea what I was going to say to him—I was certain that he was going to deck me, too.

I was a little nervous, and my palms were sweaty, but I knew this had to be done. I stepped inside and saw Brendan with three shots lined up at the bar. I walked up to him, tapped him on the shoulder and waited for the dreaded response.

"Maurice, what are you doing here?" he asked angrily. "Shouldn't you be with Stephanie right now?"

"No, I shouldn't," I responded. "Stephanie's not my concern at this present moment, but you are."

"I don't want or need your concern, bruh, so please just let me be...."

"Look, you have every right to be upset, but I want you to know that none us knew what Stephanie was doing behind your back. I definitely wouldn't have supported her behavior if I'd known."

"Come on, man, you expect me to believe that? All of you were just laughing at me behind my fucking back. I feel like such a fool."

"You're not a fool, Brendan. I want to say that I'm truly sorry about everything. I was wrong about you, but I hope we can still be friends...."

"We were never friends, Maurice, so you don't owe me anything. Look, man, I respect what you're trying to do, but I really don't want to see any of you ever again. You and your family would be a constant reminder of Stephanie, and I need to get her out of my system and move on. You of all people should know where I'm coming from."

"You're right...I respect your decision, and I understand. Take care of yourself, Brendan."

We shook hands, and I left. Then my phone rang before I could get out of the lot.

"Hey, Nikki, what's up?" I asked.

"It's your brother," she replied. "I just bailed him out of jail."

"Jail? What the hell happened?"

"He beat a guy half to death last night, and the State is trying to throw the book at him."

"Why? This just doesn't sound right...why would he piss away everything he worked so hard for?"

"The guy he beat up is the same guy who shot you in LA. This guy fronted BJ off, and he lost it."

"No, Darius Clinton shot me...what is he talking about?"

"I'm afraid not, Maurice. He admitted shooting you to BJ...it was some type of gang initiation, and you got caught in the crossfire."

"Un-fucking-believable. So, what now?"

"They're charging BJ with assault and battery, and they're charging him with attempted murder. As far as I know, the guy is still unconscious."

"Damn, do you need me to do anything?"

"No, there's nothing you can do now, but he's going to need everyone's support at his trial in about a month, though."

"Consider it done, Nikki."

"So, how was the wedding? I know my would-be-sister-in-law looked absolutely beautiful."

I paused and said, "There was no wedding, Nikki. Brendan

found out that Stephanie had been cheating on him with his friend Marc."

"Oh my God!" Nicole shouted. "Stop lying, Maurice. Stephanie adores Brendan."

"I'm not lying. Brendan punched Marc in the face and drove off, and Stephanie locked herself in their bedroom for about a half hour."

"I need to give her a call when I get back to DC and see if she's alright."

"Yes, that's a good idea. Talk to you later."

"Okay, bye."

I disconnected the call and headed home to my Dad's house. The fact that Junior now knew who shot me had sunk in. I didn't feel anger or sadness—just numbness. Junior beating this guy's ass didn't change a thing because I still had the scar on my chest to prove it. This has been one crazy-ass day, I thought.

that was tucked underneath his Eli Manning jersey.

"My name is Special Agent Greenwood, and I'm going to ask you a few of questions," he said. "First off, where-the-fuck is Lucas?"

"I don't know who you're talking about," Mike replied.

"Look dickhead," Greenwood said, "I'm gonna ask you one more time. Either you tell me where he is, or else you're looking at life in prison."

"I don't know where he is...we never have direct contact...."

"Well, you are today. Here's what you're gonna do...call him and tell him that there is a problem with the shipment."

"He's never gonna go for that...he'll know I got knocked."

"You don't have a choice. I have enough dirt on you to send you up the river for three lifetimes, son. I was gonna get your cousin to set y'all up, but he managed to jump ship. However, I'll settle on you setting up this clown with a wire."

"I can't do that...he'll have me killed. Just take me to jail."

"Look, I have exactly twenty-four hours before the powers that be pull the plug on this case, so you're gonna do what I say or else I'mma put a bullet in your fuckin' temple."

Greenwood took Mike's phone off of his hip and asked him what Donnie's number was. Greenwood then dialed the number and placed the phone to Mike's ear.

"You better give an Academy Award winning performance or else you'll be doing life in Attica, motherfucker," Greenwood said.

"Uh, what's up?" Mike asked. "We have a slight problem here."

"Then handle it, nigga," Donnie said. "I thought I told you to never call me god dammit."

"The shipment is short...you're missing at least half of the product."

"What?! Where the fuck is my dope, Mike?!"

"I don't know what happened...Juan said the shipment somehow got lost at sea."

"Bullshit. I'll be there in a New York minute, and don't you go any-fucking-where. If neither one of you tells me something I wanna hear, I'mma kill the both of you."

Donnie ended the call, and Greenwood patted Mike on the back.

"Good job," Greenwood said. "You just might have shaved off some time on your sentence."

Donnie slammed his phone on the bar where he was throwing back Black Label shots. He then motioned to pay the bartender.

"Leaving already?" the bartender asked.

"Yeah," Donnie replied, "got some business to take care of."

"Come back and see us soon," the bartender said.

Donnie gave the guy a generous tip and walked toward the entrance of the club. As Donnie was leaving, Blaze and Peanut were about to come in. Donnie inadvertently bumped Peanut outside of the door but didn't apologize.

"You can't say excuse me, muthafucka?" Peanut asked, fuming from being bumped.

"Who the fuck are you?" Donnie asked.

"Enough with the fuckin' questions, homeboy," Blaze interjected. "My man wants a goddamn apology."

"Fuck you and your man, nigga," Donnie said. "Do you know who I am?"

"Nah, muthafucka, do you know who I am?" Blaze asked.

"Fuck you!" Peanut shouted, pulling out his nine millimeter.

Pop, pop, pop!

Donnie fell to the ground after Peanut dumped three slugs into his abdomen. His eyes were wide open, and his lifeless body began leaking blood onto the pavement. Numerous screams echoed in the wind as people fled the scene.

"Come on, man, let's get the fuck outta here!" Peanut shouted.

"Where the fuck did you get that gun, Nut?" Blaze asked.

"I copped it around the block from your crib," Peanut said. "I can't get caught slippin' out here."

"I hope nobody recognized me," Blaze said.

"You're not a star yet."

Blaze and Peanut hopped in Blaze's car parked a block and a half from the club and sped off. He ran a stop sign and almost hit another car in his haste to flee the aftermath of Peanut's bad decision. Both of them had two strikes and were now facing twenty-five to life if caught by the police.

# Chapter 26

Darius waited patiently for Megan to get ready. Locating Donnie in a city as large as New York was no easy task. Mike had also proven that he was loyal first and foremost to himself, and if tested, his true colors would most certainly be revealed.

Megan stepped out of the bathroom wearing nothing but a towel. Darius looked up and said, "Let's get a move on. I wanna catch Donnie at the club before he takes off somewhere."

"I'll be ready in a minute," she said. "You're a true friend, Darren...loyal to a fault."

"Don't like the name Darius, huh?"

"No, I don't. Darius isn't who you are anymore...that person died when you changed your name to Darren. Darren is the man I love, not Darius."

"You can call me anything you want, beautiful, but I can't just forget the past."

"Nobody's asking you to forget, just move on from it. What hold does Donnie have on you anyway?"

"He had everything opportunity to roll over on me, but he didn't. He did three years because of me."

"Wrong, baby, he did three years because of himself. Nobody forced him into this life...he made a conscious decision, and now he's gonna have to live with that decision."

Megan got dressed, and they headed to the club. NYPD had the whole area blocked off with yellow tape by the time they got there thirty minutes later. People were standing around talking and speculating, and some of the officers were asking people questions about what had happened. Darius and Megan walked up to a small group of people talking near the entrance of the bar.

"What happened?" Darius asked the group.

"Somebody shot and killed the *King of New York,*" a young lady said. "Put three bullets in his ass...."

"Who's the King of New York?" Megan asked.

"You're kidding me," a young man said.

Darius already knew the answer to Megan's question and said dejectedly, "Donnie was the King of New York, baby. We're too late."

Darius grabbed Megan's hand and sauntered back to the car. Megan turned to face Darius after walking a half block down.

"It's gonna be alright," she said, hugging him. "Let's get out of here."

"That was my man, and someone gunned him down like a fuckin' animal," he said. "I never want to come back here again. Come on, let's go. Niagara Falls is a few hours from here."

"Okay, baby."

"You have a passport, don't you?"

"I have three passports in three different names."

"That's my girl."

# Chapter 27

*One Month Later*

Junior's girlfriend Delilah sat to my right and Dad to my left in the back of the courtroom. No one else could make the trial except Dad and me—Erin had just started shooting her next flick, Malik was in training camp, Gabrielle had a restaurant to run, and my stepmother was sick with the a severe case of the flu. I had been on four talk shows since the attempted hijacking—most notably The Today Show. I also landed a commercial endorsement without an agent due to my re-emergence into the spotlight.

It was day two, and things were about to wrap up. We were moments away from hearing the closing arguments after Nicole had decided to put Junior on the witness stand. She always felt that people who didn't testify on their own behalf were almost always guilty. He did a good job describing the events that took place on the night in question, and he didn't sway in his testimony once the prosecution began to grill him. Unfortunately; Blaze, Peanut and Bam didn't crack under pressure either. Even that kid Kevin was already a hardened criminal whose innocence was long gone. They all said the same scripted account of what happened that night—a stark contrast of Junior's account.

It was essentially going to take a miracle for Junior to get a favorable verdict. Mike's testimony as a character witness didn't lend much credibility because he was facing life in prison himself, so Junior was basically on his own.

I focused my attention on Junior, and he looked poised and confident. It was almost as if he knew something that the rest of us didn't. This couldn't do anything but help him in the eyes of the jurors, but I knew deep down that he had to be very worried about his impending fate. I then locked in on Blaze's lying ass sitting on the right-hand side of the courtroom, and he along with the rest of his cronies appeared to be extremely confident that Junior was going to spend a good portion of his adult life behind bars. Some friend. Bam, however, looked sullen and was withdrawal from the rest of the group. He was unconscious in the hospital for several days after the fight, but he quickly made a full recovery with no sustaining injuries other than a broken nose.

Dad looked worried, and Delilah was holding back tears. Damn, if only Nicole were able to prove that Bam shot me and that his actions triggered Junior's violent rage.

Then the unthinkable happened. The prosecution was preparing to give their closing arguments when Bam stood up and shouted, "All this shit is a fuckin' lie! I shot Maurice Ousley at that gas station, and BJ was telling the truth!"

"Order!" the judge shouted, pounding his gavel on the podium. "Order!"

"I'm a killer and a drug dealer!" Bam cried. "I can't do this shit anymore!"

"Contain him, bailiff!" the judge ordered.

The bailiff scurried toward Bam and restrained him after his complete meltdown. Everyone else in the courtroom was flabbergasted.

"What the hell are you doing, man?" Blaze asked bewilderedly. "Are you trying to get us knocked?"

Bam's purging was not only a surprise, it was the miracle that we all prayed would happen. He had been lying and scheming his whole life, and his conscience wouldn't allow him to spout off another lie. The guilt of his past transgressions had tormented his soul to the point that it altered his perception completely. He could no longer live with himself knowing what he had done to Junior and me.

"Judge, may I approach the bench?" Nicole asked.

The judge then motioned for both parties to come forward.

"What is this, counselor?" the judge asked, directing his question to the prosecutor. "You are making a mockery out of my courtroom, and I'm going to dismiss this case."

"But Your Honor," the prosecutor said.

"It sounds like Rashad Coleman made a formal admission to the court, Your Honor, and I recommend that all charges against my client be dropped," Nicole said.

"Do you have anything to add, counselor?" the judge asked.

"No, Your Honor, the State rests," he said.

"Then the case against Mr. Brent Ousley Jr. is hereby dismissed with prejudice," the judge said, pounding his gavel repeatedly. "Court is adjourned!"

Hysteria immediately filled the courtroom as Bam, Blaze, Peanut and Kevin were taken into custody by the several bailiffs on duty for perjury. Junior abruptly jumped up from the pew, and he hugged Nicole tightly before hugging Dad and me and finally before hugging and kissing Delilah.

"Oh my God!" I said. "I never would have guessed this outcome in a million years!"

"I'm thankful," Brent said, "and relieved that you aren't going back there."

"So am I," Delilah added. "I don't want to live my life without you, BJ."

"Thankfully you won't have to," Junior said. "Thank you, sis."

"You're welcome," Nicole said, "but you really should be thanking God. We were badly losing the battle before Bam's confession."

"I know, but I never lost faith," Junior said. "Come on you guys, let's get outta here."

"I'll second that," I said.

"So, what are you two going to do about your record deal?" Nicole asked. "It's amazing how Mike was able to move kilos without either one of you knowing about it. You just never know about people...."

"All I want to do is go home," Junior answered. "As for the record deal, I guess we'll cross that bridge when we come to it. Mike put us all at risk, and it cost us everything. I'm still mad as hell at him for ruining what we all built together."

"Actually, we have a new deal in place as we speak," Delilah added. "They're just waiting for you to sign on the dotted line."

"Really, baby?" Junior asked. "Who is it?"

"A small label called *Rebirth Records*," Delilah answered. "We both have artist-friendly deals that I'm sure you're gonna love, BJ."

"That's great, you two," I said.

"Yes, that's wonderful," Nicole said.

"Son, don't blow it, okay?" Brent urged.

"I won't, Dad, I promise," Junior answered.

The five of us left the courtroom and headed to the Strip House for dinner. The mood went from somber to jubilant instantly, and we were all in the mood to celebrate Junior's freedom. Man, he deserved some happiness for a change—hell, we all did.

I called Gabrielle to tell her the news, and she was elated, of course. Nicole relayed the message to Erin, and I sent Malik a text. Junior had text his mom the good news as well. Then BJ and Delilah's song played on the radio—a perfect way to start the evening.

Dinner with the family was great, and we all talked and laughed just like we had done when we were kids. We each shared with one another what was presently going on in our lives, and the shock of the evening was that Nicole had a boyfriend. They had been dating for seven months, and she was expecting a proposal very soon. Wow. Nobody even knew she was dating anybody, and now she was talking about marriage. I guess there will be another wedding in the upcoming months, and I hoped and prayed that this wedding would be drama-free.

In the following months ahead; Malik and Erin had patched up their rocky marriage, Junior and Delilah's relationship and music careers took off, and Nicole and her man set a date to be married. Erin finally agreed that Malik should sell the house in St. Louis, and they also reached a compromise regarding her spending habits. Junior and Delilah's single *Love N Pain* hit number one on Billboard, and Junior's debut album was a huge success. Nicole and her fiancé opted for a spring wedding, so the family had made plans for a ceremony in the nation's capital.

My life with Gabrielle couldn't be sweeter, and we were expecting another child. We decided to wait until the baby is born to know its sex.

As for the Watts clique, they all would have plenty of time to think about the crimes they had committed. Kevin had to spend a year in a juvenile detention center for perjury, and Sally had completely washed her hands of him. An eyewitness had placed Blaze and Peanut at the scene of Donnie Lucas's murder, so both men had two strikes and were facing life imprisonment in addition to their perjury charges. Bam was also facing a hefty sentence for perjury and his confession to my shooting. Mike had gotten a life sentence for his involvement in Donnie's drug trade.

Stephanie and Brendan had broken up, and Stephanie had begun burying herself into her work. Gabrielle had only spoken to Stephanie a couple of times in the last few months and had all but distanced herself completely from her. Brendan dissolved his partnership with Marc and formed a new company. Mr. Davison put the word out about Marc, and Marc hadn't been able to find a job or get a loan to start another company since.

As for Darius Clinton, I never heard anything about him ever again. I would occasionally wonder if the Feds ever caught up with him or if he ever let bygones be bygones as far as Gabrielle and me were concerned. I didn't hold a grudge against him now that I knew the truth about who shot me, and I hoped that he didn't harbor resentment toward us for owing him money and setting him up with the Feds. I didn't know what the future held for us, but I was certain that our lives would never be dull.

Made in the USA
Lexington, KY
31 March 2013